Advance Praise for
Fish, Soap and Bonds

"In giving voice to the homeless, Fondation creates a vision of Los Angeles on par with that of Joan Didion and Nathaniel West in its style, originality and timely urgency. His startlingly beautiful prose reflects the complicated passions behind all that is stark in Los Angeles—the best gift a city could wish for."

—Bett Williams, author of *Girl Walking Backwards* and *The Wrestling Party*

"Although set in Los Angeles in 1994, *Fish, Soap and Bonds* recalls America's anti-capitalist Thirties novels, and especially Dos Passos' *USA*. Written with compassionate fervor in multiple brief units, and including texts as various as medical reports, newspaper transcripts, police department manuals, and assorted lists and catalogs, Larry Fondation has given us what official culture prohibits: an unblinkingly close look at the poorest of the poor from the inside-out. Satire, pastiche, precise detailing, formal dexterity—Fondation's novel contains that and more—but what vibrates in the mind finally is the homeless themselves: the officially invisible made visible, and the author's refusal to avert his eyes."

—Harold Jaffe, author of *Beyond the Techno-Cave* and *Terror-Dot-Gov*

Fish, Soap and Bonds

Larry Fondation

Illustrations by
Kate Ruth

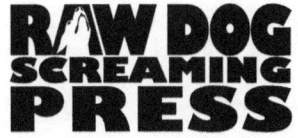

RAW DOG
SCREAMING
PRESS

Published by Raw Dog Screaming Press
Hyattsville, MD

First Paperback Edition

Cover: M. Garrow Bourke
Book design: M. Garrow Bourke
Interior Illustrations: Kate Ruth

Printed in the United States of America

ISBN 978-1-933293-37-0

Library of Congress Control Number: 2007920992

www.rawdogscreaming.com

Dedication

For Malaika, Julia and Lilly—with hope that they may both inherit and help create a better world.

Also by Larry Fondation

Common Criminals: L.A. Crime Stories
Angry Nights

Appreciation and Acknowledgements

Special thanks to Kim Addonizio, Luis Barajas, Jenna Blough, Jessica Garrison, Barry Graham, Anna Hawkey, Kathy Hayes, Hal Jaffe, Andrew Pogany, Sally Shore, Amy Turner, Bett Williams, and Eric Miles Williamson for varying kinds of help with the writing of this book. Special thanks also to Jerry, Rhonda, Rande, Donna, Robert and the many homeless men and women I talked with, whose names I should know but do not.

Grateful acknowledgement to *West* (the Los Angeles Times Sunday Magazine), *Flaunt Magazine, The Five Fingers Review* and to *Pale House* in which excerpts from the novel previously appeared.

I am especially grateful to Raw Dog Screaming Press for the publication of this novel.

A variety of sources of information are cited and "sampled" in the text. Special gratitude to: The Los Angeles *Times;* the *Concise Columbia Encyclopedia;* Peterson First Guides: *Urban Wildlife;* Realus Hill of Compton, California; the 1994-1995 *Manual of the Los Angeles Police Department*; *Webster's New World Dictionary*; *A Guide to the World of Jellyfish* (Monterey Bay Aquarium Foundation); *Pacific Currents*: Newsletter of the Aquarium of the Pacific; *The Outer Bay* (Monterey Bay Aquarium Foundation); *Image on the Edge: The Margins of Medieval Art* by Michael Camille (Harvard University Press); *The Essential Jesus: Original Sayings and Earliest Images* by John Dominic Crossan (Castle Books); "The Latin Playboys;" *Twelve Months of Monastery Soups* by Brother Victor-Antoine d'Avila-Latourrette (Broadway Books); *The World Almanac 1995*; various and numerous websites.

Finally, special thanks to any person or source that I have forgotten or failed to mention.

Special Note

Fish, Soap and Bonds takes place in Los Angeles in 1994. It is a work of fiction. The principal characters have been invented. Any references to actual people, places and events may have been altered to suit the fictional context.

Table of Contents

Part One: Skid Row

Part Two: Crown Hill

Part Three: Hollywood

Part One: Skid Row

"The somebodies will be nobodies and the nobodies will be somebodies."

(John Dominic Crossan, The Essential Jesus)

Prologue

CHIT CHAT ON THE CORNER re: the big empty, nothing, nada. The money all gone except the last drink money, way gone, Fish and Soap huddled up in unconsoled despair, the money gone again. The big radio's pumping up the volume. Raven crying because no one will buy her no more, but Bonds, on a spree, pays her $15. She still gives good head. Revived, she buys everyone a round at the Back Door Bar. The lights go on and off. Fish comes back in: "I've got good news. First time I haven't puked in three years."

The hospital is bright and shiny, then the blood turns brown. The light bulbs sit unreasonably in the sink until Bonds smashes them one by one. Everybody's screaming—the alarms are going off, the sirens, the dogs all barking. Inside the abandoned apartment, it's so quiet except the water running on the floor—an inch, two inches, half a foot—and they walk out into the desultory sun. Soap steals a lamp just for the hell of it, no place to plug it in, running fast and barefoot from the security guard, the one with the gun. The lights are blinking; the car is burning, set ablaze with gasoline by roving bands "in the line of fire."

"The whole bird's on the plate, but we just eat the feathers."

Chapter 1.
Without a Home

FISH AND SOAP ARE KISSING under the broken light bulb. The used tires are piled about twelve feet high. We have to re-arrange the glasses of water. Fish and Soap are sagging until someone stops them, "Have you got a quarter?" Fish is stunned, he's got nothing to give, and they walk some more and get stopped again, "Where did you get those clothes?" The cops carry Fish away, Soap crying, riding the Ferris Wheel after dark, but just after, a pint in her pocket. Fish out now and angry, how could you do that to me? The neon changes the color of your skin. Don't worry, they're wearing riot gear. There are several places around the state from which the H$_2$O has been stolen. Up and down the road. Flee.

Fish and Soap are swimming in a lake off the 395, near Bishop, on the way back to L.A., richer, but not wiser. One room, one bed, one couch, one lamp. It's someplace, a room, on the second floor, in the shadow of bigger buildings, heretofore, the streets, hereafter home. Fish hefts the coffee cup and hurls it at the wall, breaking it of course. Wal Mart, K-Mart, Target. Fingernails dragged along the chalkboard, teacher, teacher. Doorknobs turned, dead bolts; cowering behind the house plants. Screaming, just screaming.

Fish is standing in front of Lucy's Tacos, waiting for an offer to work. Inside, in the hills, cut the rug, lay it down, get out, no, there's no-one to drive you back; walk. The intersection of Alvarado and Sunset: burritos, walk, don't walk. The chairs are placed in a circle, the television is handing out tee-shirts, hats and other souvenirs, straight from the screen. Fish, buy me a drink. What's mine is yours. I know, but it would be so nice. It would be like a gift. I'll buy everybody a drink. Fish, you missed the point. Torn upholstery covering the wounds, blood running from the knees, down the calves, over the ankles, down the heels to the floor. Stop putting your gun on the bar, the stools, the floor. Ingredients: Tomatoes, corn syrup, vinegar and oil. Hey, who's hogging the bathroom? Fuck off. I got six beers I gotta get rid of. Piss out the window. Amorous inside, Fish and Soap enraptured, the only pleasing thing to come along.

***

Fish and Soap got married on the streets. Bonds was the best man, the witness and the minister—he'd once been a deacon in his church. He brought along a pink scarf that he'd found blowing on the street on a windy day and joked he was the maid of honor, too.

The next day they tried to file papers at City Hall to get a marriage license, but were hit with requests for blood tests and documents of many kinds. When the clerk stepped out to get the paperwork, they fled. Before they gathered at the Back Door to celebrate, they got plastic rings at a kiddie arcade. Hell, that would make it official.

Chapter 2.
Chaos Theory

THE SCIENTIFIC THEORY SETS DOWN the terms: a dynamic system with extreme sensitivity to initial conditions. Fish has got it all figured out. He drops a beer bottle on the floor of the Back Door. Angie freaks out and runs into the middle of the street whereupon she is hit by a car. She is taken to a hospital where the doctors bill the federal government a lot of money for setting her broken leg. The Senate, crying deficit, cuts the housing budget so when she is released from the hospital, the shelter in which she has been living has shut down for lack of funds. Meanwhile, the driver of the car that hit Angie was slightly drunk—though of course he had no chance to stop, she ran right in front of him. The judge didn't see it that way and threw him in jail, suspended his license.

Whereupon he lost his job because he couldn't get to it, so no money. His wife left him for the accountant she worked for as an office manager. Whereupon the driver, whose name is Fred, homeless now, walks into the Back Door and, unsuspecting, sits down next to Angie who likes him immediately and they drink together, kiss together, etc. Now Fred's fast friends with Fish who started this whole thing—and takes all the credit or blame—by merely dropping a beer bottle, which we know he did on purpose to get Angie to leave the bar; she was bugging him, kissing him, all this with Soap due to show up any minute now.

Chapter 3.
History

1. FISH HAD WORKED FOR AN insurance company. For a brief time, Bonds owned a restaurant. Soap had been married three times. Until her last trip to Harbor General, she had carried three pictures with her, one of each of her former husbands. On one she had pencilled a mustache. She had lost the pictures at the hospital, or they had taken them from her. She had no picture of Fish.

2. Fish was sitting on the floor breaking walnuts with a hammer when Soap first saw him. He said he had stolen the bag of walnuts and had found the hammer. He told her a great deal about walnuts: what a walnut tree looks like, how the crevices in the shell remind him of the human brain, how birds drop nuts on rocks to break the shells...

She noticed right off; he had big feet.

That wasn't in the hospital, but in a cheap single room hotel neither of them could afford any longer. Soap didn't know Fish to speak of back then. Just transient neighbors.

3. Though Fish had lived all his life in the city, they took him to a hospital in the desert. They said it was the only place that had available beds. He had been standing in the middle of a busy intersection in downtown Los Angeles catching cars with a baseball mitt and calling, "Yer out!," in a loud voice to passing motorists when the police took him away. Just having fun.

When they released him from the hospital after a couple of days, he had to find his own way home—along roads winding through the chaparral, the sand, the hills and then the woods.

The animals were making noises. It was night. Fish imagined he saw dead men hanging from the branches of the trees in the dark. The silhouettes of leaves looked that way to him.

He jumped at every sound, and the sounds—after a time—conjured memories of the city: owls hooting reminded him of police sirens; other nocturnal birds, of cars honking their horns at a stoplight; the chirping and croaking of insects, of creaking tenement heaters.

Fish wasn't sure what direction to walk in. He followed what seemed like the right road. At a fork, he flipped a coin.

He emerged from the woods at a 7-11. With 49 cents, he bought 32 ounces of Coke with ice. He chatted with the store clerk who knew something about owls and bats and other animals of the night. Then he went to find Soap.

4. She broke the window; he broke the door. They lived there together for a while—in a long-abandoned, fire trap of a house. Inside, the lines and marks on the floors and walls gave clues to the lives that had passed there before: scratches on the floorboards from the claws of a dog skidding to a halt; a long line on the living room wall showing how high the couch had been.

Mice were running around near the candle Fish and Soap had set up in the middle of the now-empty floor. Fish and Soap watched them with fascination for long minutes at a time. They were surprised that the mice even came out with the candle lit, but the mice went on with their rituals, unconcerned and unafraid.

5. He always noticed her hands. Her fingers were long. Her hands were shapely and had once been pretty. Then he looked again. There were scabs and scrapes. He glanced at her nose, which was also long, then back to her hands: he wanted to ask her how she managed to get her fingernails so dirty. He always kept his so clean.

6. Bonds owned a restaurant. A barbeque place in Compton. He won awards for his food. His business boomed. When they shut down the General Motors plant at Tweedy and Alameda, he lost his lunch crowd. Within a year he had to shut down. Then he went to war. Straight from the reserves. In the middle of the desert. Then he came home and had nowhere to go.

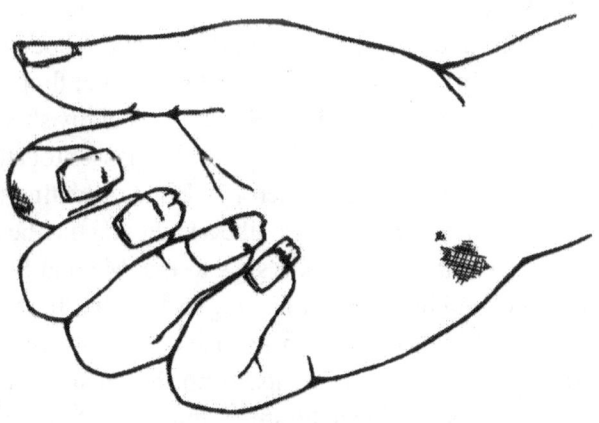

Chapter 4.
Shake It Up at the "Back Door"

THE TABLES AND CHAIRS MOVING, the bottles crashing to the floor. Animals come up from between the floorboards, scurrying around, carrying small objects in their mouths. The jukebox skips a song, then grows louder. Doo-bop. "Dance to the Music." The newcomers scream at the invasion, frightened by the invaders small but numerous. Bonds playing Space Invaders, power on, power off, pissed. "I was gonna be high scorer, I coulda had high score," over and over flip him another quarter, "That ain't the point." The regulars stay, ordering shots and beers, "Mine's all over the motherfucking floor," Overflow in the women's bathroom. "I'm so tired of fishing tampax out of the toilet bowl." Louie with the broom, swishing around the slush, the sludge, beer, whiskey, the piss on the floor, Los Angeles Iced Tea, stomping in it, splashing, packing it down, picking it up and letting it slide through his fingers, four or five now pissing outright on the floor, a woman or two squatting while the guys wave it around. Fish and Soap both laughing, but staying out of it. Fish standing up to add to the slush. Soap pulling him back to his chair. "Don't you dare." Fish, "I feel like a million bucks."

Bus full and crowded, fleeing, the asphalt sliding by like water. Chattering, disconsolate voices spun like yarn, crying, sobbing, brake hard, thrown to the floor, paramedics, nurses, run back and forth, Fish lifting injured bodies.

Soap, "It wasn't meant to be."

"Look what I got you," Fish, holding up a bright green coat, "You like it? " Sitting on turned-over trash cans, lighting butts, drinking, bright-eyed celebration. Later: languid, desultory, the sun going down, "We've got a little place to go."

New soles and heels, stitching, glue, nails, the smell of shoe polish, waiting all day, seven hours, in the shop for the job to be done, flipping through the same magazine four or five times, "Hey, Bonds, look at my shoes." Bonds, "Buy me a drink." A place called Hank's, banged their glasses together so hard they broke, laughed, "Get the hell out of here…" Bonds, wanting to give it a go, muttering with Fish's hands guiding him like a sight dog out the door. Fish: "I don't give a shit what that motherfucker says to me. Me and Soap are like this," Holding his right hand in a fist, not his fingers together but meaning the same thing—close. Bonds steaming, with no one to hold—Fish missed the cue; Bonds smashing a window with his fist from the outside, cut knuckles bleeding, the two of them racing down the street, jump over four people sleeping on the sidewalk into a fruit cart, dropping melons into the gutter, "Sorry, sorry, sorry." Blue lights flashing, blue light special—let's go to the cafeteria at K-Mart." A good, nervous laugh, chest stuttering with the effort and the adrenaline.

Chapter 5.
News Flash

Tuesday, January 18, 1994
Home Edition Section: PART A Page: A-4

EARTHQUAKE: DISASTER BEFORE DAWN; *Death, Fickle in the Ruins,* Takes at Least 33; *Victims: Collapsed apartment building claimed at least 15. A buckled freeway killed another. Many died at the epicenter, but one was 102 miles away.*

By: VICKI TORRES and JOHN JOHNSON, TIMES STAFF WRITERS

The Toll: A magnitude 6.6 earthquake, centered in Northridge, struck at 4:31 a.m. Monday. Officials reported the following: DAMAGE: Sections of several freeways and highways were closed after suffering major damage. Utility service was disrupted for hundreds of thousands of people. Damage to homes and businesses was reported as far north as Fillmore and as far south as Anaheim. DEATHS: At least 33 deaths were reported, 15 at the Northridge Meadows apartments. Hundreds of people throughout the area were injured. CURFEW: Mayor Richard Riordan declared a citywide curfew, making it illegal for people to remain on the streets between dusk and dawn.

It was, as always, the most fickle of catastrophes, bestowing death with nature's cold caprice: Fifteen from a stucco Northridge apartment building. Two from a million-dollar home in Sherman Oaks. One from Skid Row. One from the ranks of the Los Angeles police.

Elizabeth Ann Brace, mother of two, was in her home in Rancho Cucamonga, 102 miles from the epicenter of Monday's Northridge quake. Death found her anyway. When she ran to check the baby, officials said, she apparently tripped on a toy, fell and dashed her skull against her child's crib. Her husband, a gray-haired, bespectacled man, was in the next room checking on their 5-year-old son. By Monday afternoon, he said, he still had not mustered the courage to tell his children their mother is gone.

Brace's death was the most distant, but it was by no means the only one. By nightfall, the death toll from the 6.6 magnitude earthquake had reached an unofficial count of 33. At least six were victims of heart attacks. The others were casualties of chaos and its aftermath.

In the stucco-and-steel rubble that had been the Northridge Meadows apartment complex on Reseda Boulevard, firefighters had found 15 bodies by late Monday, all from the flattened first floor. Survivors said the three-story building began to collapse when the first jolts of the quake knocked out the ground-floor pilings that supported the parking garage. As the earth rolled, they said, the middle floors collapsed as if they were a house of cards. First, witnesses said, the air was filled with screams. Then it was suffused with silence. Among the youngest victims was a 14-year-old boy, Howard Lee, who had left his boarding school to visit his parents.

On the pitch-black overpass where the Antelope Valley Freeway segues into the Golden State; an LAPD motorcycle officer plunged to his death when his vehicle catapulted over a gaping hole in the buckled asphalt. Witnesses watched, horrified, as Clarence Wayne Dean, 46, of Lancaster, a 26-year veteran of the force, flew off the edge of the bridge and plummeted 40 feet to the pavement below. "His lights were still flashing and he just came tumbling down," said Andy Jimenez, 33, of Santa Clarita. "It was unreal." LAPD Lt. John Dunkin said Dean apparently did not realize in the dark that the freeway had collapsed, and he was unable to stop in time. Dean, assigned to the Valley Traffic Division, is survived by a 26-year-old son, Dunkin said.

In Room 610 of a Skid Row flophouse, a mentally ill former convict died without a witness to say whether it was an accident or a suicide. Jose Hernandez either fell or jumped from his open window when the Frontier Hotel at Main and 5th streets began to sway. Authorities did not discover his body until about 15 minutes later, when security guards began to evacuate the establishment. Police said it appeared that Hernandez, a transient in his 40s, was taken by surprise when the building began to shudder and that he fell accidentally. But the manager of the hotel, where he had stayed off and on since November, said Hernandez's parole officer had described him as unstable; he speculated that the man had "panicked and jumped."

On a canyontop cul-de-sac in Sherman Oaks, on a street known for its breathtaking views, Mark Yupp, a 31-year-old entertainment industry executive, and his 32-year-old fiancee, Kerry, were found dead in what was left of their down-stairs bedroom. Police said the two were apparently asleep when the quake uprooted their hillside home. Beams and wiring, furniture and concrete were scattered for more than 100 yards down the slope from the house's founda-tion, punctuated in two spots by the wreckage of their cars, a BMW and a Porsche. More than a dozen neighbors, barefoot and shivering, tried to rescue the couple, digging frantically with their hands. But when aftershocks hit, they said, they were forced to run to safety. Only the couple's whimpering puppy survived. "Someone yelled up the street in the darkness, 'Dial 911! The house here went down the hill, the cars, everything!'" said Chuck Mitchell, 53, a retired sheriff's deputy who was staying in a nearby house. "We all ran down there with our flashlights, but we couldn't see anything. The house was totally gone."

Nearby, in the 3600 block of Beverly Ridge Drive, another mountainview home was knocked off its stilts and down the side of a canyon, trapping and killing a 4-year-old girl. Bert Lockwood, a neighbor whose own home sustained consid-erable damage, said it took firefighters about two hours to scramble down the hill and cut through the debris with chainsaws to free the home's owners, Stas Vigil and Nancy Tyere. But it was not until midmorning, he said, that rescue workers were able to locate their daughter, Amy. Lockwood said he watched sadly as the workers wrapped the little body in a blanket and took her away. "You could look down the hill and see teddy bears and pink blankets," he said. The child was the youngest known casualty late Monday, authorities said, but they warned that the toll probably will rise.

Emergency workers said Monday that it will take as long as two weeks to clear the debris from the spot where the Antelope Valley Freeway collapsed onto the Golden State and to unearth any vehicles that might have been crushed there. And several of those injured at Northridge Meadows remained in criti-cal condition Monday night. Meanwhile, as night fell, coroner's investigators continued to increase the death toll: a Chatsworth man who was fatally struck on the head by a falling object inside his mobile home. A 45-year-old man in the Fairfax area who also suffered a fatal head injury. A 92-year-old woman who died in a trailer fire in Northridge. And a 25-year-old Sherman Oaks man who was electrocuted when he touched a wire.

As coroners' investigators struggled to identify the dead, survivors grappled with the devastation of sudden loss. "I have a hard time explaining how she fell so hard," said Brace's stricken husband, Thomas, 49, standing red-eyed in the pastel living room of their four-bedroom Rancho Cucamonga home. Surrounded by a litter of Aladdin coloring books and baby toys, Brace seemed stunned as he recounted the particulars of their life. He and Elizabeth, he said, had married late and had moved from Lomita to the Inland Empire because they could afford a bigger home and she could afford to become a full-time homemaker and mom. "Everything was exactly as we had planned it," he said. "Except we didn't plan this morning." They were in bed, he said, when they felt the jolt. They waited a moment before rising to check on the children. He went to their daughter's room while she ran to check on their son, 17 months. He heard a thump, he said, and found his wife unconscious near the crib.

San Bernardino County Coroner's Deputy Monika Padilla said an autopsy is pending, "but from the looks of things, it looked like she just hit the crib the wrong way—like it was just one of those freak accidents." Her husband was at a loss for words. Asked to describe his wife, he looked blankly at a reporter. "I loved her very much," was all he could say.

The Los Angeles Times

Chapter 6.
Tossed

"WHAT YOU MEAN? I AIN'T going no fucking place." They're throwing Bonds out on his ear, kicking and screaming, Fish trying to help, they've known each other so long.

Bonds: "They don't want my black ass in there—" shouting: "Fuck you, assholes, fuck you!!" Fish: "C'mon, Bonds, no sense getting fuckin' killed." Bonds, with a beer mug in his hand, they're out of their own neighborhood, stealing, it's stealing, cops pat down, banging on their balls, "Where you get this beer mug?" Push and shove, rough him up a little, nightsticks, a loud hit on the shoulder, the beer mug crashing to the pavement, Soap sees them, runs up crying, scared, the weather: starting to rain, just a slight bit like a splash, cops knocking down Bonds, shoving Fish. Soap gets there, cops gone, Bonds and Fish bleeding, but not bad. Soap's got a pint, them walking off, Bonds in the middle, "Let's get a kick out of it."

Chapter 7.
Piso Mojado

THE DONUTS LINED UP UNDER glass like tin soldiers in a case, hooking up the hoses to the water and the syrup, Coke and Sprite and Root Beer running, coffee dripping through the filters like a leaky roof dripping muddy water, shaping the dough, dropping it in the grease, the timer buzzing, out, drain, smearing chocolate, licking fingers against the law, a job, it's a job, a long time since that happened, edgy and impatient.

Chapter 8.
Criminal Justice or Snickers

SOAP IN THE COURTROOM, STANDING, sitting, Bonds pulling her down into her
seat. The judge in black robes. "Just as soon could've been white robes," said
Bonds, hassled at the door, through the metal detector, patted down, shaken
down, taken down, buttoned down—"You can go now." Pepsi cans, smoke, the
corridors, saddest place this side of the hospital.

Bonds tells Soap his story while they wait for the case to be called: "Even
in California never seen so much fucking sand. Motherfuckers said nobody
was killed. Bullshit. They just don't count the dark ones. Ask the Iraqi women,
they'll tell you all the fucking nobodies killed," Bonds talking on, getting
louder, cussing more until some son-of-a-bitch in a suit comes by, "Is he bothering you?" Bonds furious, but quiet, keeping a lid on it, clenching fists inside
the pockets of his pea-coat, but Soap all up front: "Who the fuck are you?"
The ass-hole in the suit retreating, gone, disappearing in her assault, the guy
vanishing into the men's room, Bonds laughing, hugging Soap. "I hate these
places, see..."

Soap put the money in, but it wouldn't come out and she punched the
buttons again, but nothing, not the Snickers bar she wanted and punching the
numbers, angry, she said out loud "fucking thing," and kicked it once and
it was almost time to start inside again and Soap shouting louder, kicking
harder, no Snickers bar, the Marshall coming over, "Lady, put a lid on it," but
undaunted, "I want my money back." "Lady, calm down." "Who do I see to
get my fucking money back?" "Lady, there's a phone number on the vending machine, the court has nothing to do with it," "Well, that's bullshit, there
should be somebody—a real person—you can talk to give you your money
back or you shouldn't have the fucking things here." "Lady, calm down or I'm
going to throw you out of here," "Oh, fuck off," Bonds came running out of
the men's room. "What's going on here?" Kids gathered around watching the
Marshall pick Soap up under the arms. Bonds, "Hey, put her down." "Oh yeah,
who the fuck are you?" Now two Marshalls, now three, down the off-white
corridor, down the tile floor, down to the elevator bank into the lobby and onto
the street, never seeing Fish get sentenced to 90 days for public drunkenness,
never seeing it again, the judge, stenographer, the hard wooden benches, the
men in uniform.

Chapter 9.
Roman Catholic

BEFORE SOAP: "HOW MUCH IT cost?" Ave Maria. What's salvation?

The carnival's bright lights beckoning like pheromones, like hormones, how you supposed to be saved like that? If you supposed to be pure, how come cats go into heat? Tell me that. If you're born with original sin, where does it come from? Don't give me any of that Adam and Eve shit, I just want to come, to get my dick wet, it's been such a long fucking time. Don't tell me it ain't right, giving her twenty dollars, paying the motel by the hour, stretching it to two hours, another twenty bucks, don't tell me nothing, it's just like buying a candy bar, just like buying a pair of pants. I just want to get off, get fucked, get laid, to dip it, to pork her, to fornicate, her with the big floppy tits, her willing, her selling it for twenty bucks, and I do her once, I do her twice, met at the Midway, her naming her price, me a hundred bucks in my pocket, 20 for her, 20 for the motel, 20 for rides and games, 20 to keep—the whole thing harder to pull off than buying a gun. Kyrie Eleison.

Chapter 10.
Sacred Fire

I DON'T KNOW. I WENT to the counter and I ordered and they asked me questions and then I repeated my order and they asked me questions again and I said, "My name is Fish," and they laughed and I repeated myself again and then I said the same thing and finally agreed and they agreed and I got in and I ordered but they ignored it and then I repeated myself and we went through it again and finally it was over and then I saw Soap and she, walking with a halter top and hot pants and she had her nails done, both hands and feet electric pink, and I got down and kissed her perfect toes and kissed her perfect lips and I was Fish and I said Fish is in love, and I'd never talked about myself in the third person but here I was and I kissed her again and again and again and then the bad thing happened and Soap said I was unclear and I asked her what she meant and she tried to say but didn't and I repeated it again and we went back and forth and finally we made up and it was like Christmas it was like New Year's it was like sacred fire and once again it was only pleasure, it was, it was, it was.

Orange with shadows, hot. "Fish, he went back in, all the way and..." "Don't talk about that shit, Soap. How many times have I told you?" Fish and Soap and Bonds were walking, hot and sweaty, it was a long walk, and it was from the bus and they got off the bus and they walked, they were walking to the beach, hot and sandy with soda and beer cans and cigarette butts and the man on the Palisades asked them for money and Bonds laughed and Fish wanted to fight and then to make a deal, they'd knock off the guys selling oranges and take all their money, who'd give a fuck, but Soap started to cry, "How could you?" and Bonds agreed with her, Fish calling them "moralistic sons-of-bitches," Bonds laughing at the language, then: "You've become a cold motherfucker." That's when Soap started in about Fish going all the way in, all the way in to get him, then back out again, burns on 20% of his body, the boy did, and Fish with his hands and his arms, "You should have seen them, and he wouldn't stick around for the newspaper guy." "Shut up, Soap."

Then that's when it happened for the first time: the sun dropping down like a ball dropped from a tenement roof, the purple coming over the sky, the approaching darkness like a headache, like knowing when you go to bed, you'll be hungover in the morning, waking up over the Pacific Ocean, still talking to the man. Fish wanted to fight, then to cut a deal. Fish said, "I'm into deals, but that's it with the arguing," with the clouds like UFOs, with the Italian tile laid out at their feet, with Greek columns rising beside their legs and torsos and chests and Soap's big tits and their arms, that's when the clubs, the handcuffs, the shouted words out of nowhere, Bonds catching it in the face, but this time, the first time, Bonds bleeding, but this one time, Fish getting the worst of it, clearly, bones breaking, clearly blood, his words, his attitude, "Fuck you, fuck you, fuck you, fuck you…" Bonds stepping in, taking it on the shoulder, the back, the back of the head. Then, no arrests, just gone. Blood, the unbroken pint, ministering to Fish, church/shelter on Arizona, Christian concern, "oh, you poor thing," but Fish smart now and silent, taking all the help he can get, "oh, thank you, kind Miss," her clean fingers and manicured nails feeling good on his skin as she washes, cleanses, bandages and gives him directions to Santa Monica Hospital, a place he'll never see.

Chapter 11.
The 49 Cent Taco

THE PRICE OF THE TACO has dropped to 49 cents and Lupe does not get her raise. She puts in the meat and the cheese and the lettuce and she wraps the taco in paper and she puts it in the bin and after an hour, she gets $4.25 less taxes. A man pulls up in a Mazda, walks in and orders three tacos to go. Lupe's colleague, Sam, who also makes $4.25 less taxes, for an hour's work, rings up the order, Lupe filling all three tacos, Sam bagging the food, taking the money, $1.60 including taxes, making the change, 40 cents out of two one dollar bills, the guy leaving the restaurant, climbing back into his Mazda, driving away. These tacos cost 49 cents, only 49 cents, just 49 cents. No-one else sells tacos for 49 cents. Fifty-nine cents is next cheapest taco in town. We know that we can buy a taco for forty nine cents because we pay Lupe and Sam just $4.25 an hour, that's what makes a taco so cheap, what makes the executive fly to Washington to say to the Senators, "Don't raise the minimum wage." "Don't make us pay health benefits." We all know how much we need a 49 cent taco.

Lupe is raising a child, the child's name is Guillermo and they call him Memo and she has $4.25 an hour times 30 hours a week times 52 weeks a year to buy what Memo needs and we know how much we need a 49 cent taco.

In two weeks time, Bonds will buy Lupe a drink at the Back Door Bar.

Later that night, Fish on purpose and deliberately with pre-meditation and forethought, by planning, forecasting, etc., walking into a foreign place, another bar, another neighborhood, wooden sticks in hand, broken pool cues that is, swinging wildly, aiming at no one, but at things, at objects, crashing lamps, glasses, bottles, video games, everything in sight, hitting no one, breaking everything in sight, smashing, trashing, doing it all, whirling, swinging, no one reacting, no one stopping him, Fish laughing, having a good time, a great time, having a grand old time, like an earthquake, breaking glass, high-pitched sounds, the owner's dog finally coming out of the back room, charging, teeth bared, Fish knowing the game was up, the ball game over, fleeing, slamming the door right in the dog's face, yelping, right in the snout and Fish away, running away, faster than darkness.

Chapter 12.
Rabies

rabies or ***hydrophobia,*** *acute often fatal, disease of mammals, caused by a virus transmitted from an animal to another through infected saliva, usually through a bite. After a variable incubation period, rabies produces fever, headache, nausea, and pain at the site of the bite, followed by convulsions, inability to drink fluids (hence hydrophobia), apathy, and death. A vaccination of rabies vaccine is administered to the bite victim to prevent the disease from developing.*

The Concise Columbia Encyclopedia is licensed from Colombia University press. Copyright @ 1989, 1991 by Colombia University Press. All rights reserved.

Chapter 13.
Rabies II

HE GOT BIT BY THE dog, got bit in the leg, got bit not once, but twice, didn't seem bad, seemed to heal pretty quick, just a little infection, forget it, but then all of a sudden, the fever, the onset of fever, the splitting headache, taking down the pictures from the walls, no lakes, no oceans, no water, no H_2O, no fluid, no liquid, nothing wet, screaming out loud, so loud, very loud, piercingly loud, then not at all, no water, softer, then not at all, H_2O, no H_2O, then County General, tubes, the whole bit, the whole scene, the whole 9 yards, it's a miracle he survived.

Chapter 14.
Rabies—Public Health Version

How is rabies transmitted?

Rabies is most often passed from animal to animal, or animal to human through bites. The rabies virus in the attacker's saliva (spit) is passed through the puncture wound into the victim's skin. The virus can also be transmitted by licking when a sore or wound is exposed to saliva from an infected person or animal.

Thus far, in the U.S., the vaccine has never failed to fight off rabies. There have been instances in other parts of the world where the vaccine has failed because it was not given properly or in a timely way.

Is there a shot that can be had BEFORE a bite?

Yes, it is called the pre-exposure vaccine. It should be had by anyone who comes in contact with wild animals in an area where rabies is a problem. For example: veterinarians and staff; animal control officers, varment hunters; spelunkers (people who explore caves); people who plan to travel to countries where rabies is a problem.

How would I know if an animal had rabies?

There is no way to know without having a live animal or its carcass laboratory tested. Do not attempt to guess. Assume it does if you have any reason to suspect that the animal is rabid.

Suspect any hair bearing animal that behaves in an unusual way, appears or behaves tame or untimid, does not take flight when approached by a human or domesticated animal, does not assume behavior that is consistent with normal instinctual self preservation.

What are the symptoms of a human having rabies?

In humans, it can take as little as nine days or as long as a year or more for the symptoms of rabies to appear. Most people who get rabies, however, begin to show symptoms of the disease within 60 days after being exposed.

It is very important not to wait for symptoms before seeking care. Rabies travels from the brain to the nerves and travels up the nerves to the brain. The virus usually takes several days to begin attacking the fine nerves nearest to the bite or exposure site. If rabies gets into the nerves, vaccination is useless.

The earliest symptoms of clinical rabies infection in humans are pain, tingling or numbness at the site of the bite, fever, sore throat, nausea, vomiting, diarrhea, abdominal pain, and feeling tired and "run down."

Some sufferers show early signs of the virus getting into their brain and nervous system. They feel anxious, are fearful of things with no clear reason, they are agitated, nervous and may be depressed.

As the disease gets worse, it does so rapidly. In a matter of days a person can become paralyzed, have spasms in the throat, see hallucinations, go into coma, have heart beat problems and then die.

The most important thing to remember is that if someone is exposed to a possible source of rabies, that modern rabies treatment, if it is started in time, allows our bodies to fight the virus and avoid the disease.

(Taken from America OnLine)

Chapter 15.
Bucket

HE COULD NOT FIND THE bucket. He had the mop and the cleaner, the ammonia-based cleaner to clean and shine the floor, he had the source of water, tap water, not hot, but a free flow of water. He did not have a bucket. He did not have money. So the obvious solution was out of the question. He could not go to K-Mart, to the hardware store, to the supermarket, anywhere, to buy a bucket. He decided to go out to the corner and ask for money, to panhandle, as they call it, he did not see it that way, what does that mean anyway—panhandling? whatever it's called, he would ask people, strangers, people he did not know, strangers, he would ask them for money, just a quarter, 25 cents. He figured a bucket would cost him six dollars, just 24 quarters, how long could it take? The first nine people did not answer him, walked right by, straight ahead, not a word. The next three people, all, every one of them, each single one to a person gave him some change, not all quarters, but change, coin, small currency, totaling 92 cents, better than a quarter a person, a net take of almost $.31 per person, $5.08 away from purchasing a bucket. Then a dry spell, ignored again, cast aside, no never mind. This is where Bonds comes in, why they're so close, why Fish feels as he does, because Bonds comes along, "Man, what you doin' here?" "I'm trying to get enough money to buy a bucket." So Bonds comes through, comes up with a five spot, right there, five bucks, "Let's get out of here, Fish, let's go buy that bucket."

Chapter 16.
Roll of Film

IT WAS WRONG. WE HAD it all wrong. In the picture. She was on the left, wearing red. Not in the middle, not wearing blue. It was a different picture. Fish knew it and argued and wondered and the guy at the one-hour photo spoke no English but Fish couldn't believe it because it was not just that a picture was lost, not just that they lost a picture, anyone can do that, it's easy if you handle hundreds of photographs; maybe you put one in the wrong package someone else gets it amidst their photos of Florida, "Hey, who the fuck is this?" They say, getting a good laugh, Fish with his fingers in his mouth, then they get to Soap on the left wearing red, "Hey, this lady's kinda cute," Fish proud of her looks even though her eyes are starting to droop a bit. But that's not the thing, not now anyway. Now, the issue's the picture, though in blue and in the middle, she—not she, not Soap, this has got to be someone, not Soap, but it's Soap, it is, it really is, looks like she did in San Diego, way back, young then, tile, Spanish tile, falling off all the roofs, back in San Diego, back then, when it was the first hook-up, the first connection with Bonds, just out of Camp Pendleton, just out of the Marines, just ending service to his country, after all that, after the Reserves, after the restaurant, after the Gulf War, but before the street, seems like such a long time ago now, no computers, no faxes, driving a tank a whole different proposition. Soap, not wanting to look at the picture. "Something's not right, maybe it's a bad omen or something." Bonds laughing, but gently, "You ever think some guy's just playing with those camera-computers late at night, maybe fuck with the pictures just to fuck with your head," Soap wanting to cry but holding back and Fish now excited, now almost jumping up and down, "Let's go. We got some money, so let's go to K-Mart, this goes in a frame…"

Chapter 17.
LA, I Could Have Burned You Down

EVERYTHING'S ON FIRE AND THE fire runs up and down the hills like a great dragon, like a monster, and all I had to do was wake up before dawn and put a box of matches in my pocket. If the embers catch, it could take out whole towns—Arcadia, Monrovia, Altadena, La Crescenta—no more foothill towns. A conspiracy, a plan, an act of terrorism, a plot, a cabal of arsonists, firebugs, pyromaniacs, destroyers of property. Lack all human decency. "What kind of person would do that?" These beautiful homes, 4000 square feet, throwing furniture into the swimming pool.

Chapter 18.
The Suspect

A TRANSIENT, A HOMELESS MAN, dressed in hiking boots, shorts, a sweatshirt. "He looks like he's from Eugene, Oregon." He's dirty, cold, without shelter, without money, without means, he cannot afford it, no dinero, he doesn't have a pot to piss in—he's been apprehended, taken into custody, arrested, booked, taken in for questioning, on TV, on radio, his picture in the papers...

Chapter 19.
Fish, Soap and Bonds

"HEY, LOOK, IT'S BARRETT!"

"It was just an accident. I was just trying to keep warm."

"He feels so bad: 'I didn't mean it, I didn't mean to, I didn't, I was only trying to keep warm, I was only trying, I was only trying....'"

So they have Barrett Day at the bar. They got banners and balloons and little hot dogs to serve at the Back Door, Old Milwaukee, free from 4 to 6, then a buck a bottle, no one stopping at 6 p.m., 6 o'clock, no one stopping then, continuing on, the party continuing, balloons popping, only three out of 50 of them left with air—then by 10 o'clock, a 20 gallon trash can full of empties, Old Milwaukee, nothing else. No windows or pictures on the wall, blue and red lights, shouting again, Bonds and Fish in the thick of it, little do the cops know who the party is in honor of, the sign saying "Barrett" long since taken down in the ruckus, no injuries this time, no arrests, quiet it down, shut it down, the end of the night.

Chapter 20.
Pretty

FISH AND SOAP, AT IT again. One more time. Deja vu. Just like before: the bottles, the screaming, the cussing, just like the good old days; Bonds trying to quell it, to stop it, re-direct it—Bonds ever patient, Bonds solving problems, Bonds the diplomat. "What's this all about, this fucking fight, this goddamn argument at three in the morning, that's gonna get us kicked out of this place, this one room, this first night we've spent indoors in three weeks. What the fuck's the matter with you guys? We got 100 bucks, better than ever, well maybe not ever, but better than in a long time, impressive even, for us, I mean."

"Soap wants to spend 20 bucks on a make-over at May Company, so I said, 'What the fuck, are you nuts?' and she started to cry so then we started throwing things and I ain't backin' down, 20 bucks is one-fifth of all we got and what the fuck they gonna bother with some homeless bitch over at May Company, they're only doing it on the cheap 'cause they want you to buy a shitload of cosmetics and we ain't got the cash for that and we sure as fuck ain't got no credit cards so I say fuck it, it's a bad idea, like flushing good money down the toilet."

Bonds: "We could just split the money three ways or thirty-three bucks apiece and each one of us spend ours however we want to..." "Yeah, and she blows hers on a fucking make-over and I get stuck dropping 30 of mine on this fucking dump and she stays here anyway so then where the fuck am I?"

Bonds: "I'm not pushing it."

Soap: "We got 100 bucks. It's Monday. Right now we can stay here 3 days. If none of us do shit with this money, we'll still be out on the streets on Thursday. If we all go have a good time, we'll be back on the streets tomorrow. Big fucking deal."

Fish: "Don't scoff at 2 nights indoors."

Soap: "This place is a shithole. There's more bugs in here than there is in most doorways."

Bonds: "She got a point."

Fish: "Oh shit, all right. We owe 30 for tonight. We all agree on that, right? So we get 23 bucks apiece plus an extra dollar, which I'm keeping. Administrative fee." He passes out the money. "I'm putting mine toward tomorrow night. If you all get another 10, you can stay here with me."

Chapter 21.
Apple Pie Story

FISH: "ME AND MY BROTHER were just kids. We were at Clifton's and it was late and Herb went through the line and stole a piece of apple pie. He just marched over to this long table and sat down and started to eat it. I was busy looking at this old woman with huge tits. I whistled at her and she scowled at me like she thought I was making fun of her. You know me, man. I was serious. I thought she looked hot.

"Herb had taken one bite of the pie and was spitting it back on the plate. He got right up and huffed over to the counter and asked to speak to the manager. The manager came over to Herb and asked what he could do for him. I still remember this: he called Herb "sir." Herb looked right at him and he kept a straight face, I don't to this day know how he did it. And, he said: "This pie is stale." He held it up chest-high like it was a plate of Holy Communion. The manager started in with all these apologies and Herb just looked at him and said, "I am never, ever going to steal a piece of apple pie from this place again" and he walked out. The manager looked at me and said: "Are you with him?" I didn't say shit, but I was about to burst out laughing so I just hit the door as fast as I could. And, I had *paid* for my food…That was Herb for you…"

Chapter 22.
Germs

SUMMER HAS ITS GERMS, ITS pests, winter has its own. On slides, under microscopes the detective scientists call their shots: transmitted by mosquito, airborne, "it's in the water." Something's always there.

Tissue samples, biopsies, blood tests, urine analysis: "she's a carrier," "the test is positive," "the prognosis is not good," "for someone who's homeless, he's pretty healthy."

Nicotine, carbon monoxide, toluene, benzene, etc.

Leaving the apple on the table: first mealy, then discolored, soft, decomposed; it begins to smell, to corrode; it is quanta of debris, particles, slush on the table and finally worms crawling on the wood.

Chapter 23.
Bacteria

bacteria *microscopic, unicellular organisms having three typical forms: rod-shaped (bacillus), round (coccus) and spiral (spirillum). The cytoplasm of most bacteria is surrounded by a cell wall; the nucleus contains* **DNA** *but lacks the nuclear membrane found in higher plants and animals. Many forms are motile, propelled by movements of a filamentlike appendage (flagellum). Reproduction is chiefly by transverse fission (**MITOSIS**) but conjugation (transfer of nucleic acid between two cells) and other forms of genetic recombination also occur. Some bacteria (aerobes) can grow only in the presence of free or atmospheric oxygen; others (anaerobes) cannot grow in its presence; and a third group (facultative anaerobes) can grow with or without it in unfavorable conditions, many species form resistant spores. Different types of bacteria are capable of innumerable chemical metabolic transformations, e.g.* **PHOTOSYNTHESIS** *and the conversion of free nitrogen and sulfer into* **AMINO ACIDS**. *Bacteria are both useful and harmful to humans. Some are used for soil enrichment with leguminous plants (see **NITROGEN CYCLE**), in pickling and alcohol and cheese fermentation, to decompose organic wastes (in septic tanks and the soil), and in* **GENETIC ENGINEERING**. *Others, called pathogens, cause a number of plant and animal diseases, including* **CHOLERA, SYPHILIS, TYPHOID FEVER**, *and* **TETANUS**.

Chapter 24.
Hot

FISH GOT A FEVER, "ONE-oh-four," Soap says, though they don't have a thermometer, she's holding her palm up against his forehead, holding it up, taking it off, her hand, bitten nails, feeling the fever through her fingers, her other hand rubbing his cheek, gentle, while Bonds paces, walks back and forth, crunching needles and glass and cans underfoot in the vacant place, the walls missing, gone, chopped down or covered with graffiti.

"Gotta go, gotta get him over there, this thing keeps going up." Bonds and Soap ready to carry Fish across the river, over the bridge, giving him the last of the stolen Tylenol, such a long walk to County General up Main, past Union Station, along the tracks, past the projects, the abandoned warehouses, the old dairy, the Mexican restaurants, the hospital a behemoth building on a hill.

In the waiting room. In the waiting room. In the waiting room. In the waiting room. In the waiting room. Uninsured Uninsured Uninsured Uninsured In the corridor In the corridor In the corridor. Steal more pills. Two hours, four hours, six hours. 8 p.m. 10 p.m. midnight, by two o'clock the fever broke, Fish covered with sweat, shaking some as the body fought, pulled through, his shirt wet, his hands wet, his hair wet.

Chapter 25.
Prettier

SOAP GOT HER MAKE-OVER, got eyeliner and eye shadow and blush and foundation and lipstick and two or three squirts of a spicy kind of perfume. She sat in the chair at the counter, in the middle of the May Company cosmetics department, the staff a bit skittish at first, Soap "obviously homeless" or too poor or out of it or something, despite the morning shower she snuck in at the Y, but, hey, she had the bucks, the cash, two tens and a five, and she plunked down her twenty five dollars, which included a tip—they had to do it, hesitating, halting, but looking at each other knowing one of them had to, they couldn't refuse, she had the money, she was a customer, Soap knowing it, too, until finally a young Asian woman, hair slicked back, pasty cheeks, red lips and long red nails, stepped forward in her Estee Lauder smock: "Let's do your colors."

Chapter 26.
Memories of T and A

IN THE BAR HE LIKED her ass. In the tight jeans, no underwear. Tartan. Tartar. Tonga. Sparse crowd. She walks by, over and over. Then the place fills up. He sees her less, lost in the crowd. Guess. Jordache. Levis. Sees her less. Infrequently. Unobstructed view. Her ass no more, so much so that's it's only a glimpse. She's in the middle, in the midst of it all. Dim lit—songs playing, not live. Just a box. Swallow a couple of pills, it'll be alright. Wet tee-shirt contest; no shit. The one with the biggest tits wins.

Chapter 27.
Luck and History

SHE QUIT SMOKING.

She got fat.

Not quite so simple really. It never is.

She dyed her hair. She bought a dog.

She got divorced, became homeless.

All these unconnected...except the last two of course.

Like all of life: un-relations, synapses, disconnections, then—all of a sudden—intense collisions and embraces, scattered and plural, like splattered glue binding random, unintentional surfaces:

Fish.

Bonds.

Though not one of them had anything to speak of, Soap knew what she had in Fish and Bonds, and she suspected they knew, too.

Despite their dispute, Soap knew that Fish would find her particularly pretty with her pale purple eyelids, her blush and mascara, her passionate, near-lavender lips...

Chapter 28.
Temp

1. Moving furniture from one office to another
2. Demolition of a condemned building: stacking bricks
3. Cleaning box cars on a freight train
4. Sweeping floors
5. Mopping up after a flood at Union Station
6. Removing rubble after the Earthquake
7. Cleaning out a chemical storage tank
8. Loading trucks
9. Unloading trucks
10. Scraping paint

Chapter 29.
Parallel Events

ROBBING THE STORE. ROBBING. THEFT. Several ways. The lone gunman. Ski mask or not. Smart enough to take out the video camera. Roy is a part of it, waiting outside, waiting to drive the car. Roy got caught. Someone wrote down the license plate number. Roy did the time alone, never snitched. Roy is a friend. Roy once went with Soap, but Fish doesn't know it. Then there's the group method: a collection of bit parts, really. Ten or twelve people. Walking into the store at the same time. A 7-11. The owner: small, Pakistani, turbaned. At first he protests — verbally, then with gestures, threatens to call the police. It takes all of five minutes — the removal of all items in the store that can leave in pockets and bags; alcohol and soda and dog food and diapers — the destruction of all equipment — soda machines, display racks, the microwave oven; one young man asking for the owner's turban, punching his face, breaking his nose, to get it; the dispersal of the whole crowd. The arrival of the police a few minutes later, finding no one, nothing except the owner clutching a paper towel to his bleeding nose.

Chapter 30.
Mercado

FISH AND SOAP ARE AT the market. They have $22.19 and they are buying groceries. Some other customers are giving them shitty looks. Fish and Soap are paying no attention. Instead they are arguing about splitting packages. For example, they both want juice boxes. But Fish wants Cranberry juice; Soap wants Cactus Cooler. Fish suggests that they tear off two cartons each from the existing packages of six. Soap thinks that this is wrong, that it is not right, that it is breaking the rules, that they will get in trouble. Fish tells her, in no soft voice, that he thinks her position is ludicrous, why should you buy six juices when you only want one, just because the company that made them says so? He points out Coke and eggs, both of which can be broken down into smaller groups of product, like splitting atoms. Soap says that juice boxes are different because the packages are wrapped in plastic and are not made to come apart. Who will buy the loose ones? she asks. Fish begins to talk louder and louder and finally the manager, who had given them a dirty look in the first place, as if he were itching to find a pretense to throw them out, comes over to them, a security guard in tow, and asks them to leave. Fish, who ordinarily argues those kinds of things, is tired today, tired in body, tired of arguing with Soap, so he says, "come on, honey," and puts his arm around Soap and heads for the exit.

Chapter 31.
Paralysis

"ONCE I LOST THE RESTAURANT, man, shit just spun out of control. I dropped into the crapper, bro. Before—in the morning—I'd be up at the produce mart by Five AM Sharp! I'd be downtown, showered, dressed, natty. Man, I was on a roll. But after the place got closed, I couldn't even get up in the motherfuckin' morning. It'd be noon before I could get my will up to get out of the goddam' bed. But, shit, at least I'd get up in the PM and hit the streets, look for a fuckin' job. Then, when I didn't get no offers—nothing more than minimum anyway, not even five an hour—I just lost my heart.

"Then the fucking war. You know, getting called up. In a way, I thought that'd save my ass. I was focused as a motherfucker over there, not doing nothing, but some kind of routine at least, you know waking up, three meals a day. Fuck, I guess prison'd do the same shit for you.

"Anyway, when I got back, you know it just hit rock fuckin' bottom. Used to be that I could shit, shower, and shave in fifteen minutes, get some cologne slapped on. Then something happened to time, man. I'd get up and shit and have a smoke, and I'd look at the fucking clock and half a fuckin' hour would be gone. Vanished. Damn! Then brushing my teeth, the same fuckin' thing. Half hour, an hour. Just at the sink. A whole motherfuckin' hour. Got worse and worse, man. Up at noon: an hour to shit, an hour to shave, an hour to shower. Be three o'clock. Then four. Then dark. And I'd say, "what the fuck, man, ain't no use now. It's fuckin' nighttime and all the places'd be closed." So I'd just turn on the tube. Just veg, nothing. Couldn't even tell you what shows was on. Staring at the goddamn screen. Barbara'd come home and there I'd be. Doing nothing. She tried to understand at first, but, shit, I got worse. Wouldn't even shower or shave. Couldn't. Just nothing. She had to throw me out.

"Out here, I had to get my ass in gear. I got cut, slashed in the fucking arm, my first night on the streets. I can take care of myself now. But, hell, that was three years ago, and I'm still fuckin' here. Shit..."

Bonds took a deep breath. Bonds had seen Fish cry, but Fish had never seen Bonds cry. Fish wanted to keep it that way. Bonds had his head in his hands.

"Let's get some fuckin' beer," Fish said.

Chapter 32.
Placita

FISH LEFT BONDS AND SOAP at the bar. He'd had enough for one day: probably not enough booze, but enough talk and chatter, enough endless dreaming and scheming—at least until tomorrow.

It was late on a Sunday afternoon and Fish hadn't been to Mass in years. But all of a sudden he realized his strong desire to leave the bar was accompanied by a siren song to go to church.

On the grounds of the church, everything was for sale, but in a good way. Some things Fish recognized—tacos, melon slices, plastic statues of the Virgin, candles in tall glass cylinders painted with pictures of the Sacred Heart, the Crucifixion, the Assumption, the Ascension. Some things he could not ascertain—foods: antojitos, sesos, lengua; obscure objects he assumed were religious: medallions and epaulets of varying kinds; productos Latinos: medicinal herbs in Baggies, potions in bottles, Uñas de gatos...

The courtyard was packed with worshipers and buyers, diners and vendors, large packs of children—the girls mostly in dresses, the boys in white shirts, some in ties—running all over, men with bedrolls who seemed to have spent the night, and, everywhere and ubiquitous, the rhythms of Spanish, only Spanish, joyful mostly, pero Español solamente.

The Mass, of course, was in Spanish, too, but Fish, an old lapsed Catholic, knew exactly what to do, when to kneel and sit, when to stand. Fish picked up the missal and tried to sing the songs but he couldn't pronounce the words. He tried anyway. Some kids around him giggled, but in a friendly way. Fish laughed and made funny faces at them—friendly, too. Their parents did not protest their laughter; they smiled warmly at Fish.

Fish, eyes closed, listened hard to the sermon, but it was tough to follow and fleeting: corazon, Jesus, Maria, padre, dinero, los pobres, salario minimo, justicia. He knew he agreed. He could tell by the sounds and by the reaction of the crowd. The place was packed, standing room only.

Fish put all his money in the collection, all he had except his special quarter, which he'd had for a long, long time, and which he'd never spend or give away, never.

He left, as he planned, with joy.

Chapter 33.
Rwanda

FISH IS AWAKE. Soap and Bonds and a couple of guys they just met are all cuddled together in a ball for warmth. They sleep in the doorway of an abandoned building, a place long vacant and convenient in its way, near the corner of 3rd and Main. Fish is hungry, but he does not want food. He is thirsty, but he does not want a drink. He wants the paper, the news, the *LA Times* most likely, but any paper will do, the *Daily News*, *The New York Times* sometimes, but it's always yesterday's, so that's no good, he wants the latest news. He does not want to read about Los Angeles, or about California, or the national news; he wants stories from Rwanda, the tragic conflicts, the Hutu and the Tutsis, the genocide, the worst news anywhere in the world; he keeps up with it every day, searching frantically for the morning paper—in trash cans, in doorways, walking up towards City Hall to find a vending machine, quarter in hand if he has one, otherwise asking each person whose path he crosses—"Can you spare a quarter?"—it has to be a quarter; the machines don't take nickels and dimes. He hates asking for money; Bonds showed him how, some technique, but he is still bad at it, hates it, gets most of his money from GR and sideways, from friends; Soap would share with him, and Bonds, and Barrett, whoever, he always gets by, but no one understands his newspaper thing, and how he needs it right when he gets up, first thing, when no one has any money, having spent it all the night before, the last bottle of Night Train, Mad Dog, Wild Irish Rose, and a late night taco or hot dog or nachos from 7-11. When he finally gets a paper, his hands tremble, shake, unsteady with excitement, today cold, too, and stiff; he looks for stories about Rwanda and Burundi. He caught the first breaking news: the plane crash that killed both country's Presidents. Shot down over Kigali, the Rwandan capital. Then the flood of violence, the killings, the genocide. His interest was not prurient. When he read the stories, he cried. Fish could care deeply about the Hutu and the Tutsis, but he couldn't explain it to anyone without crying. Bonds had seen him cry—once or maybe twice. Fish got up early—he even had a battery-operated alarm clock for awhile until it got stolen—so he could do this all alone. He wished he could do something, to make a difference; they, so desperate and in need; worse off than him. He wished he could matter.

Chapter 34.
Two African Presidents Die in Plane Crash

KIGALI, RWANDA—The presidents of Rwanda and Burundi were killed in a plane crash near this capital city's airport Wednesday as they flew back together from regional peace talks in Tanzania. Rwandan diplomats charged that the plane was shot down.

Presidents Juvenal Habyarimana of Rwanda and Cyprian Ntayamira of Burundi had been in Tanzania for a meeting of east-central African leaders seeking ways to end ethnic violence in the two countries.

Rwanda and Burundi have been racked by bloodletting between the rival Hutu and Tutsi ethnic groups. The deaths of the presidents, both Hutus, are almost sure to inflame tensions in both countries.

*(**Los Angeles Times**, Thursday, April 7, 1994 From Times Wire Services)*

Chapter 35.
Guards Hunt, Kill Premier in Rwanda

WASHINGTON—Marauding presidential guards terrorized tiny hapless Rwanda and killed its prime minister and almost a dozen Belgian peacekeepers Thursday in a chaotic, murderous frenzy of revenge for the deaths of two Central African presidents.

Shortly before she was hunted down, Rwandan Prime Minister Agathe Uwilingiyimana told Radio France International: "There is shooting. People are being terrorized. People are inside their homes lying on the floor. We are suffering the consequences of the death of the head of state."

(Los Angeles Times, Friday, April 8, 1994 by Stanley Meisler—Times Staff Writer)

Chapter 36.
Conversation

BONDS RAN INTO FISH AT the corner of 2nd and Los Angeles Streets. He looked especially grim.

"What's up, homie?"

"Shit. What do I look like, one of the Beastie Boys? We're too damn old for that kind of fucking talk."

"You're only as old as you fucking feel."

"Fuck you."

"What'd I say? Shit, I feel like I'm ninety."

"Fuck."

"You're depressed, man. Let's get a drink."

"No. You go."

"Come on, man. Over to the Back Door."

"I'll pass."

"What the fuck's wrong with you?"

"Shit, I ain't even got a dollar, man."

"Why you not say so. Man, I got money today."

"I know. I heard. I don't want to take your green, Bonds."

"Oh, come on."

"I usually got something."

"You usually do."

"Not nothing, anyhow."

"Where you hear about my money from?"

"It's getting around."

"Shit."

"What happened?"

"Some white motherfucker in a suit gave me forty fucking dollars."

"No shit."

"Man, and you know, I don't even ask motherfuckers in no suits for nothing. I give them the fucking pass over, man. But this guy looked different or something. Bullshit, I was just fucking desperate. I'd of asked any sorry ass fucker that walked by…"

"Forty dollars?"

"Yeah. Shit, man, I thought he wanted me to suck his dick for it or something, you know? I was gettin' ready to hand it back to him if he opened his fucking shit ass mouth."

"What he say?"

"That's what gets me, man. Nothing. He didn't say a fucking word."

"Shit, maybe he stole a bunch a money from work or something and felt guilty or some shit."

"Shit, I should try to find the fucker again. Maybe he's out wandering the streets feeling guilty. I can say, 'Man, I'll soften up your white guilt. For a fucking hundred.'"

Fish started to laugh hard.

"Maybe the bills are fucking marked…you spend 'em. You get arrested. He walks."

"Fuck you. Let's go spend some at the Back Door. Johnny wouldn't fucking know if they was Monopoly money any fucking way…"

At the bar:

"You remember the first time you had nothing? I mean when you knew you were wiped the fuck out. Busted flat? The first time?"

"What kind of fucking question is that?"

"I mean, you had money before. So did I. We weren't always broke. You remember when it dawned on you, 'man, I ain't got nothin.'"

"Shit, I guess so. It seems like another fucking lifetime."

"No shit."

"It was after I lost the restaurant…."

After a couple of drinks they stopped talking. The Lakers were on TV.

Chapter 37.
Dirty Bathroom

FISH WALKED INTO THE BATHROOM AND IT WAS A MESS. MOST
PUBLIC RESTROOMS WERE BAD; THIS WAS HORRENDOUS, BUT HE
REALLY HAD TO GO.

"WHAT A FUCKING STY, GODDAMN," FISH SAID.

SOAP WAS WAITING OUTSIDE.

FISH WENT BACK OUT.

"I CAN'T SHIT IN THIS FUCKING PLACE—IT'S DISGUSTING."

"WHERE THE FUCK ELSE ARE WE GOING TO GO—SAK'S FIFTH
AVENUE?"

"YOU KNOW HOW MANY PLACES WE'VE GONE—HOW LONG WE
BEEN HOMELESS NOW—THREE YEARS?—BUT I'M TELLING YOU,
SOAP, OUT OF—WHAT MAYBE—THREE HUNDRED BATHROOMS—
SHIT, MAYBE MORE, MAYBE WAY MORE—YOU KNOW WHAT I
MEAN—THIS IS THE WORST, THE ABSOLUTE FUCKING WORST."

"LET'S TRY TO GO SOME PLACE ELSE THEN…"

"I'M NOT GOING TO MAKE IT…"

FISH RAN BACK INSIDE AND BEGAN TO CLEAN UP A LITTLE SO
HE COULD EVEN BEAR TO SIT DOWN.

THE FLOOR HAD SO MUCH OVERFLOWED WATER AND PISS ON
IT—TWO INCHES DEEP—THAT IF HE DROPPED HIS PANTS THEY'D
IMMEDIATELY GET SOAKED. HE HAD NOTHING TO MOP UP THE
LIQUIDS WITH SO ON THAT ONE HE JUST ROLLED UP HIS PANTS.
THE TOLIET BOWL WAS CLOGGED UP AND FULL OF PISS AND SHIT
AND PUKE THAT WOULDN'T GO DOWN. HE WENT OUTSIDE AND
GOT A STICK AND TRIED TO SHOVE IT ALL DOWN THE TOILET
BOWL—HE WORKED AT THIS FOR A FEW MINUTES ALL THE WHILE
HE REALLY NEEDED JUST TO GO HE THOUGHT HE WAS GOING
TO LOSE IT IN HIS PANTS. HE MADE THE MISTAKE OF TRYING TO
FLUSH. THE WHOLE MESS GURGLED UP TO THE TOP OF THE BOWL
AND OVERFLOWED IT—FISH RUNNING OUT OF THE STALL—THE
ONLY STALL—WITH NO DOOR—AND OUT OF THE WAY OF THE
ONCOMING SHIT AND SLUDGE FLOWING LIKE LAVA AND HE OF
COURSE LIKE A CITIZEN OF POMPEII FULL OF FATE AND DOOM.
WHEN THE SLIME STOPPED COMING AT HIM HE WENT BACK INTO

THE STALL FOR A SECOND RUN AT THINGS. HE NOW KNEW HE COULD NOT DO A FUCKING THING ABOUT EITHER THE FLOOR OR WHAT WAS IN THE BOWL SO HE'D CONCENTRATE HIS EFFORTS ON MAKING SURE THE SEAT WAS SOMETHING HE COULD SIT ON.

THERE WERE NONE OF THOSE COURTESY SANITARY SEAT COVERS OF COURSE—HE WAS LUCKY THERE WAS TOILET PAPER—SO HE COULDN'T JUST PUT A BARRIER BETWEEN HIS ASS AND THE SEAT. IT WAS GROSS—ALL PISS AND PUKE AND SHIT ENCRUSTED ON BOTH SIDES OF IT. HE WENT TO THE SINK—NO PAPER TOWELS—THE TOILET PAPER WAS THIN AND CHEAP SO IT CLUMPED WHEN IT WAS WET BUT IT WAS ALL HE HAD SO IT WOULD HAVE TO DO—HE WIPED AND CLEANED LIKE IT WAS HIS MOTHER'S HOUSE AND WHEN HE WAS DONE HE WASHED HIS HANDS AND WIPED THEM TOO ON THE CHEAP TOILET TISSUE AND HE SHOUTED OUT TO SOAP "THIS AIN'T THE RITZ BUT NOW I CAN SHIT IN PEACE" AND HE KEPT TALKING TO HER AS HE SAT THERE SHOUTING AT THE TOP OF HIS LUNGS BUT SOAP COULDN'T HEAR HIM SHE WENT INTO THE LADIES' ROOM WHICH WASN'T HALF AS BAD AS THE MEN'S WOMEN BEING A LITTLE NEATER AND ALL FOR THE MOST PART BUT IT WAS NO PALACE EITHER AND SHE HADN'T LOST HER SENSE OF DIGNITY YET SO SHE WAS GOING THROUGH THE SAME ROUTINE AS HER PARTNER JUST HAD READYING HERSELF FOR THE INEVITABLE, THE ONLY AVAILABLE, ETC.

Chapter 38.
At the "Back Door" (I)

"DID I TELL YOU ABOUT that time I was selling insurance?" Fish asks.

"Yeah, Fish," Bonds says.

"It was this lonely housewife. I felt like I was in that movie, you know, the guy who wrote 'The Postman Always Rings Twice,' he wrote the book...?"

"James M. Cain," Bonds says.

"Yeah, that one."

"'Double Indemnity.'"

"What?"

"That's the name of the movie."

"Right. Well, she was like this pretty blonde chick and her husband was out of town."

"How'd you end up there?" Soap asks.

"Jeez, Soap," Bonds says.

"Right, I mean, you know, we don't go to peoples' houses no more. So, no, she made an appointment. She came to see me."

"At your office?" Soap asks again.

She's heard it all before, too, but she's going along, acting like she's hearing it for the first time.

"She kept crossing and uncrossing her legs," Fish says.

"Did she have an anklet on?" Bonds asks, going along now too.

"Yeah, yeah, she did," Fish says.

"Just like in the movie?" Bonds asks, smiling slyly.

Soap shoots Bonds a look.

"I mean, I was trying to figure out what was going on. She kept on flirting and I kept on flirting right back. And she signed on the dotted line—biggest policy I ever sold. She gave me a check right then and there."

No one said shit. They knew the next line, therefore they knew how the rest of the night would be.

"To tell you the truth," Fish says, tired from his own monologue, "She never fucked me. And her check bounced. And so did three other of my customers. All the same fucking week. Two days later, well, you know the story, my ass got fired—"

Chapter 39.
In the Middle End

IN THE 2ND STREET TUNNEL all bright and lit and tiled walking west with hope and hopefulness following a lead on a job some work a livelihood an occupation a vocation a calling, call it anything you want to: a possibility an opportunity a chance a new chance a way to go, a way to conquer to subdue to get around at least the decade of the greedy and the needy—pumping gas at the UNOCAL the gas station on Glendale Boulevard just down the hill from Dodger Stadium, one of the first ones maybe, where cars line up just after a game to fill their tanks for the long ride home to Orange County—checking oil washing windows power steering fluid all of the above Fish convincing himself it was a holy act like going to apply to seminary—"I'm going to be a fucking priest" he had said to Soap—a long walk through the bright tunnel across Beaudry past the lake at Echo Park stopping but only for a while to watch the tall geyser of fresh water pumped into the air the paddle boats circling the plume of wetness the Asian water lilies and the red bridge the idyll broken by the sight of graffiti on the walls across the street he'd read of the gangs in the paper that toll in counterpoint to the new church rising on the other side of the lake—he walks past Burger King and McDonald's on his left and there it is, his sanctuary his refuge he fishes the help wanted ad crumpled out of his pocket dirty and frayed and checks the address he knows this is it butterflies in his stomach it has been so long "Can I speak to the manager?" he mumbles straightening his hair with his fingertips as he speaks as clean as he can be given the circumstances but standing tall for sure upright good posture his gym teacher had said that about him in high school. "I'm sorry, we filled that job this morning…Try us again. We usually have some turn-over in the summer." Walking back the same route looking so decrepit now so luminous just a few minutes ago now so gray and dim and profane cut south on Beaudry this time walking east back so far got to go to Central Avenue wishing for a beer wine whiskey something but penniless no dinero nada not even a soul on the street to beg from to proposition to ask for a nickel a dime a dollar east and east on 3rd Street, the 3rd Street tunnel so gray no tile so dim no lights to speak of anyway so tired so different a gray dreary lifeless tunnel long and echoing—suddenly fear and a little shaking not from no booze but scared you could die here and no one would know—heart attack stroke mugging knifed shot beaten who knows—and Fish begins to run, run, run emerging on Hill Street the light in his eyes Soap would be waiting, Soap, Soap excited in anticipation meaning to mean well in asking "how did it go?" not expecting to tap into the downer the depression the shit after the shower—could he go somewhere else avoid her for now come back tomorrow yes that was it he could find something else that was not the only job in Los Angeles it's a big city quite the town the city of lights surely…surely something surely there'd be something surely there'll be something—he thinks maybe Soap has enough for a drink so we can plan map out the future decide how to spend the money I'll have tomorrow decide where to go a fresh start where to drive the car…

Chapter 40.
Fight

BONDS CUFFED ONE OF THE other guy's ears but he took one on the jaw himself. Soap had wanted to stay and help, but Bonds told her to run, that he'd be alright, that he could take down these two guys, that anyways it was her they were after, intent on rape, sexual assault, forcing themselves on her. At worst, all they'd do to him was kick his ass. "They can't really hurt me," he said. Soap looked in his eyes. She could see his seriousness and intensity. Reluctantly, she ran off as fast as she could.

Bonds was lucky in a way. They were in an alley. There were dumpsters. He found a stick. He swung it wildly, like a madman, all his rage concentrated in the smooth arc of the wood swooshing in the night air. He heard the sounds of the stick hitting the two men—soft tissue and hard bone—and the sounds of the men crying out. He continued to swing.

The mens' shoes crunched gravel and broken glass as they ran away.

"We know who you are. We're gonna get you!"

Bonds looked at the stick before he threw it away.

Blood stained both ends.

Chapter 41.
Moving

WHILE BONDS AND SOAP SLEPT, nestled in doorways in Chinatown, away from
the Row, Bonds keeping himself scarce for a bit after the fight, quiet and silent
for a time, at least while the whole thing blew over, which he was certain it
would in no time, Night Train doing what it does to the memory—hell, it could
be all over now for all he knew—while Soap and Bonds and downtown slept,
Fish was scouting, doing the reconnaissance on, looking to find, a new place to
live, a new neighborhood to call home, new surroundings to settle down in, the
lack of a structure, a house, an apartment, a domicile, notwithstanding. They'd
be moving—west, he was sure; he was certain of that, no doubt. Yes, going
west. Out of downtown. Away. Towards the sun. Away.

Part Two: Crown Hill

"The center is dependent upon the margins for its continued existence."
                    (Michael Camille, Image on the Edge)

Chapter 42.
The Other Los Angeles

LOS ANGELES IS LUSH WITH bougainvillea and camellias nourished with water stolen from the Owens Valley. Los Angeles is a swimming pool in the backyard and a BMW in the driveway. It is a restaurant on La Cienega all abuzz at the entry of Sharon Stone or Madonna. It is the upcoming "Trial of the Century," one of many, hordes of media at the Criminal Courts Building, for arraignment, for preliminary hearing, for jury selection, and in Brentwood, morbidly filming "Nicole's" condo. Los Angeles is the beach, the surf, the sand. Sunshine.

We are not there.

Los Angeles is the drop-beat of rap and the break beats of hip-hop. It is gunshots in the Compton night. Los Angeles is bank robbers dressed in body armor. Criminals. Hyper-violence. Noir.

We are not there.

Los Angeles is El Pueblo de Nuestra Senora la Reina de Los Angeles de Porciuncula. Now located on Cesar Chavez Boulevard, nee Brooklyn, the signs all in Spanish, lively, energetic, salsa music blaring from boom boxes made in Korea. Or kim-chi, barbecue and indoor driving ranges in Koreatown. Or the sounds of Jazz in the Crenshaw twilight, jerk chicken wolfed down at Coley's before camping out to hear Billy Higgins still play the drums, just a few miles due west of the old Central Avenue haunts.

We are not there.

We are sitting in lawn chairs on an empty lot on Miramar, near Third, just west of downtown, the Field of Dreams across the street, full of soccer players in the setting sun, another group less skilled playing down on Lucas at the entrance to the old Belmont tunnel, LA's first subway notion.

We are at Lucas and Miramar, on Crown Hill, just west of downtown L.A. They were going to call this "Central City West"—skyscrapers, hotels, fancy restaurants. Then the bottom fell through. Speculators paid $80 a foot for land. Now they can't sell it for $30. So it stays empty—acres and acres, right in the heart of the city—waiting for a rebound in the market.

The Mayor flattened one parcel—an acre out of a hundred—and made it into a soccer field. They call it the "Field of Dreams." Nothing else around. After ten at night, it all belongs to the homeless. For most of the day too, for that matter. In one of those ironies of L.A. in the 90's, the Chamber of Commerce has just built a multi-million dollar new headquarters directly across 3rd Street, anticipating a trend that never happened. Yet, anyhow. Just wait. This is Los Angeles—City of Change.

Fish and Soap and Bonds and about five more of their friends are sitting amidst the weeds in dilapidated lawn chairs, telling stories. Fish goes, then Bonds goes, then Soap gets in. They all have stories. The three of them are the most vocal. They are leaders, they have clout. The others mostly just listen and laugh.

They are all having a good time when the patrol car arrives. The "Crown Hill Eight," scamper and scatter; none get caught. But the police see the make-shift tents of scrap canvas and homes of cardboard and plywood. Under orders, they proceed to tear the dwellings down. They kick the flimsy structures, eight people's homes. They kick with their boots. They use their batons; they dismantle with their hands—they pile everything—weed, canvas, cardboard, the contents all in a pile. They radio for the Department of Public Safety to send a truck to come pick it up, to haul it off. The cops wait a few minutes.

Fish is behind some bushes, not ten yards away. He hears them talking. One cop feels good about it—he feels he has done his job. The other one feels bad. Ironically, the one who feels bad showed the most vehemence in trashing their shelter and their stuff—venting his frustration, perhaps. Maybe his wife fucked some other guy last night. Who knows?

"I can't sleep after nights like this," he says.

"Fuck it," the other one says.

"We don't need to stay here waiting for Public Safety," the first one says.

"Those guys are napping some fucking place anyway," the tough cop says.

They get in their car and drive away.

The "Crown Hill Eight," come out of hiding and rebuild their homes. Fish is mad, kicking and screaming.

"Chill, man," Bonds says.

"Yeah, Fish," Soap says. "I wanted to re-decorate anyway. Gives me something to do."

Bonds, "Shit, I was just pissed thinkin' I'd have to listen to that sad-ass apple pie story for the 31st fuckin' time."

"I wish we had a hammer," Fish says.

Chapter 43.
History of Los Angeles: Homicide

LOS ANGELES HAS A HISTORY, but no one knows it. Those who do think it started with the movie moguls—Louis B. Mayer and Jack Warner as founding fathers.

People lived here a long time ago—the forebears of the Gabrieleno—but no one knows who they were.

The first known resident of Los Angeles—La Brea Woman, the star of the George C. Page Museum—was a homicide victim, clubbed over the head and tossed into pits of tar 9000 years ago. Some things never change.

Chapter 44.
Bathroom Tale

FISH: I GOTTA FIND A BATHROOM.

Bonds: There's one right there.

Fish: You ever been in that fucking hole. Smells like shit, piss all over the floor, never any toilet paper…

Bonds: OK, let's go to Gus's.

Fish: Yeah, Gus's is fine. They're cool. Don't have any paper towels, though.

Bonds: Shit, who the fuck are you, the Craig Claiborne of public fucking bathrooms?

Fish: I hate those air dryers, man. You can never get your hands dry.

Fish starts to walk faster.

Bonds: You running at Hollywood Park?

Fish speeds up even more.

Fish: I gotta go…Hey, who the fuck is Craig Claiborne anyhow?

Bonds: You read the paper. Restaurant critic for *The New York Times.*

Fish: I don't read the food section. What you want to read that shit for anyway. All that good food you can't afford.

Bonds: I don't read it no more. That's back when I had the restaurant.…

Fish and Bonds got to Gus's. It was pretty quiet, mid-afternoon. They trudged through the patio. There was a pretty but lost-looking woman alone at one of the round tables. She had bleached blonde hair with lots of black roots; she was eating soup. She raised and lowered her head with each spoonful, and when she looked up, Bonds could see her bright green eyes, a little glassy, but gorgeous.

Bonds: I'll wait right here.

Fish: Get us some coffee, man. It's cheap here.

Bonds: OK, but I don't want to lose my place.

Bonds laughed. He was sitting two seats from the woman, but they were still the only two on the patio.

When Fish got back from the bathroom, Bonds was sitting with the bleach-blonde, his arm around her shoulders.

They chatted a while, the three of them. She spoke in riddles, Fish thought. Our Lady of Perpetual Confusion.

Chapter 45.
Soup

ON CROWN HILL, ON THE hill of the kings, the crest of the city, the commanding
heights — vacant, abandoned, strewn with the belongings of Fish and Soap and
Bonds and all the others, poor and discarded; on this hill, at Bixel and Miramar,
in this place, their new home, this crown of thorns, Soap began a tradition, a
practice, a new venture–regular and ritual, lauded and fabled, notorious in a
way: she began to fix a Sunday meal, the first Sunday of every month, just like
when she was growing up and going to church, First Sunday — a meal to share.
Something simple — it had to be. Something that goes a long way, something
traditional. She made a great big pot of soup. She went to the produce district
and charmed her way to bagsful of fresh vegetables, a day old, a little wilted
and spotted, but who would care- swimming in soup, they'd taste just fine. And
something else, something, Soap could change what she cooked, provide some
variety, the spice of life — minestrone, lentil, navy bean, chicken. Soap knew
she could get some meat.

The crowds came from all over. Soap started to make soup every other
Sunday. She thought of stealing some large pots, cauldrons, but she didn't
know where to get any, and besides rumors spread so quickly, soon one of
the missions donated a giant pot and Soap had practically to light a bonfire,
hanging the pot from a stick like a witch's cauldron. Albeit a good witch, in
order to cook in such quantities, and for one and all. The large pots brimmed
with vegetables and sometimes meat, though not the best cuts of course — but
nonetheless, food, nourishment, a wholesome meal. Inside the cauldron, a
full delineation, a declension, a conjugation, a kingdom of vegetables, like
a post modern Linnaeus of flora-root vegetables — because they were getting
old and turning brown, and soft, giving way to spring and all, still the others
and the regulars — celery and carrots and green beans, and the constants, like
potatoes — except during the famine — so long ago, but so now — a tomato
base, onions, garlic, a dash of oregano, donated in quantity by Smart and
Final, along with, of course, salt and pepper, stolen from (Shhh!) the very
same Smart and Final on Fig., no one looking. All in all a classic vegetable
soup, with the garlic and the oregano, an Italian flair — a minestrone!! The
word spread...

From antiquity on, soups have always held a very prominent place in the daily life of monasteries. This is still true today, particularly in French monasteries, where soup is often served twice a day, for the dejeuner (lunch) and, even more appropriately, for the souper, as the evening meal is called in France. The appeal of soup is a universal; it seems to be almost of a basic instinctual nature. Soups are always welcome anytime of year, hot during the cold winter months, and cold during the hot weather. I have always noticed with the guests who arrive at our monastery, how comforted they feel after a bowl of homemade soup is presented to them. It seems an anticipation of the warmth and peace they hope to find during their stay at the monastery.

(Taken from Twelve Months of Monastery Soups *by Brother Victor-Antoine d'Avila-Latourrette. New York: Broadway Books. 1998)*

The television stations came, then left; donations poured in, then vanished,

Soap, determined, kept it up for three months. Finally, her energy left: no more Sunday Crown Hill feasts.

Minestrone De Verdura
(Tuscan Green Vegetable Minestrone)

Ingredients	*6-8 servings*
3/2 cups olive oil	*10 cups water*
large onion, chopped	*2 potatoes, peeled and diced*
2 carrots, sliced	*small raddichio, chopped*
2 celery stalks, sliced	*1 cup white wine*
1 15-ounce can of cooked cannellinni beans	*1 bay leaf*
	chopped parsley
1 15-ounce can peeled tomatoes	*salt and pepper to taste*

1.   Gently sauté in olive oil the onions, carrots and celery stalks for about 5 minutes. Add the beans and tomatoes and continue sautéing for 2 more minutes.

2.   Add water and bring the soup to a boil. Add the diced potatoes, raddichio, wine, bay leaf, parsley, salt and pepper. Cover the pot and simmer for 60

minutes. Turn off the heat and let the soup stand for 15 minutes. Remove the bay leaf. Serve hot. Grated cheese may be sprinkled on top of each serving.

(Taken from Twelve Months of Monastery Soups *by Brother Victor-Antoine d'Avila-Latourrette. New York: Broadway Books. 1998)*

Chapter 46.
Girlfriend

BONDS HAD HIMSELF A GIRLFRIEND. It had been a while. He was happy. He bought a round of drinks. But she looked puzzled all the time. Fish couldn't look straight at her. Not without laughing at least. To Soap, he called her, 'Our Lady of Perpetual Confusion." Bonds learned about it and got mad. Fish tried to brush it off, "It's a Catholic thing."

Chapter 47.
The Observatory

WORKING OUT OF THE HOME Depot parking lot on Sunset and Western, Fish gets paid for a half-day after working a full one. No recourse available.

He walks hard up Vermont, past the taco stands and street vendors, past the pierced and tattooed crowd, past the rich peoples' houses north of Los Feliz, past the Greek (he'd never seen, never could afford, a concert there, though they all stood in the parking area one night, with Bonds, listening to Al Green, his favorite singer, and now theirs, too, until the cops, tons of them, told them all to take a hike), trudging up through the tunnel to the Observatory. Fish walks to look out over Los Angeles, to be—for a minute—King of the Hill. He looks out at the Hollywood sign, at the big homes in the hills, at downtown and the skyscrapers. He's depressed. He feels like shit. He sees the bust of James Dean. He's alive.

It is hot so Fish ducks inside the Observatory to see the exhibits—about the moon, about the weather, about Mars. He realizes how little he knows. He puts a couple of bucks in the donation jar and leaves. Fish trucks back down the hill to find Soap and Bonds and Our Lady of Perpetual Confusion. He'll join them at the Back Door and buy them a drink. He still has a few bucks left in his pocket.

Chapter 48.
Walking Distances

SOMEONE GIVES SOAP A PEDOMETER

Crown Hill to MacArthur Park   1.1 miles

Crown Hill to 2nd and Main   1.2 miles

2nd & Main to the Back Door Bar   1.3 miles

Chapter 49.
Bathroom Fixtures

THEY ALL BECOME EXPERTS ON various kinds of bathroom equipment. They play trivial games—Who can name the most brands? Which ones work the best? Leak the least? Here are the top 10:

1) Sloan
2) Kohler
3) American Standard
4) Bobrick
5) Chicago
6) Delta
7) Moen
8) Price Pfister
9) NuTone
10) Briggs

Chapter 50.
Midnight at Taco Bell

PISO MOJADO. DON'T DRINK THE water. Peligro! Peligro!

How do I? Walking. How do I, running? How do I? How?

Here one minute and gone the next. That's how she is. I suspect her with everybody, the fucking whore. With Joe and Mike, with that little piss-ant social worker who comes around with meal coupons, free fucking baloney if we only listen to some asshole preach Sodom and Gomorrah for an hour and a fucking half. (With Bonds even).

I want a fucking taco. Cerrado. I want a burrito. Cerrado. I want a fucking tostado. Fucking cerrado. I got a buck and a half, but it's fucking late. At least they let me piss. But fuck'em. No tacos. I piss on the floor. The fuck thinks I'm going to anyway. Why he's standing outside with the mop when the floor's already "piso mojado." Like I don't know fucking Spanish.

Where the fuck is she? Where? I want her back. I want her now.

Chapter 51.
Simpson Held after Wild Chase

O.J. Simpson, the football great who rose from the mean streets of San Francisco to international celebrity, was arrested Friday for the murders of his ex-wife and a male friend after leading police on a gripping, two-hour chase through the rush-hour freeways of Southern California.

The dramatic capture of one of the best-known and best-loved public figures in America came shortly before 9 p.m., about 10 hours after he was to have turned himself in to Los Angeles police. Simpson's lawyer, Robert L. Shapiro, said Simpson, 46, had agreed to surrender earlier, but bolted at the last minute with Al Cowling, a longtime friend and former teammate at U.S.C. and with the Buffalo Bills.

A massive manhunt involving scores of law enforcement officers ended in the cobblestone driveway of Simpson's Tudor-style mansion, as Los Angeles Police Department officers in bullet-proof vests converged on the white Ford Bronco in which Simpson and Cowlings had fled.

As the truck sat parked, its hazard lights blinking silently in the balmy June night, Cowlings got out of the driver's seat and walked into the house. Then, for nearly an hour, a distraught Simpson sat inside the truck, reportedly cradling a blue-steel revolver and demanding to speak to his mother.

Hundreds of supporters gathered in the upscale neighborhood, chanting "Free O. J.," and rocking police cars. Meanwhile, the LAPD Special Weapons and Tactics team and negotiators surrounded the house, eventually coaxing Simpson out of the vehicle by cellular telephone. He put the gun down and emerged about 8:50 p.m. carrying a framed family photo.

Simpson went into the house, used the bathroom, called his mother and drank a glass of juice, authorities said. He was then transported by police motorcade to Parker Center for booking and transported to Men's Central Jail. Cowlings was booked on suspicion of harboring a fugitive. He was being held on $250,000 bail.

The dramatic arrest, broadcast live on national televison, capped a tragic week-

long drama that began with the slayings of Simpson's ex-wife, 35-year-old Nicole Brown Simpson, and Ronald Lyle Goldman, a 25-year-old Brentwood waiter whom she knew.

Nicole Simpson and Goldman were found stabbed to death early Monday morning outside her Brentwood condo. Police sources said the two were slain sometime after 10 p.m. Sunday as her two small children slept inside.

Although the Police Department had refused all week to label Simpson a suspect, and Simpson's lawyers said he was innocent, sources inside the LAPD made it clear from the outset that he was the focus of the investigation. The former college and professional football star was briefly handcuffed and taken to headquarters for questioning. He was later released, and remained free as evidence mounted against him day by day.

By Friday, detectives had concluded their case, recommending that Simpson be charged with two counts of first-degree murder. The charges, which include a "special circumstance" of multiple killings, could bring him the death penalty if he is convicted.

Los Angeles Police Cmdr. David J. Gascon said Simpson had been scheduled to turn himself in to police at 11 a.m. Friday, with arraignment scheduled for that afternoon in Los Angeles Municipal Court.

But 45 minutes, and then an hour, ticked by and Simpson was nowhere to be seen. Finally, just before 2 p.m., police held a news conference to announce that Simpson had officially become a fugitive.

"He is a wanted murder suspect," Gascon said tersely, "and we will go find him."

It was unclear how the 6-foot-2, 210-pound Simpson—who had been dogged by crowds of reporters and cameramen for most of the week—had managed to escape authorities, who had felt confident that someone so famous would never attempt to flee…

*(**Los Angeles Times**, Saturday June 18, 1994. By Jim Newton and Shawn Hubler— Times Staff Writers)*

Chapter 52.
Still Looking

EVERY MORNING, FIRST THING, As usual Fish would rummage frantically and in great haste for a newspaper. Hard to find at 6 AM. No one through with it yet. No, not in downtown. Now, harder to find. Now, not in so many places.

But Fish would look all over, in trash cans, at bus stops, by the union head-quarters on Bixel, by the Chamber of Commerce, all the way back at Phillipe's, against fences, in the alleys, in parking lots.

As soon as he found a paper, Fish would look for just one thing—Rwanda: not on the front page, scrambling through the front section, towards the back pages, no cataclysm today apparently, always better when he can get the news magazines, too, more detail, some of the time anyway. Today will be foreign reactions, the UN, more hand wringing; Fish sits down on the curb and cries.

Bonds: What's up?…Oh, you got the paper…

Fish tried to hide his tears from Bonds at first, then it became obvious and he would openly cry, look up at Bonds, "Don't tell Soap," and let the tears roll down his cheeks, but he wouldn't talk about it, explain it, say a word, just look into Bonds' eyes and let him watch him cry.

Chapter 53.
Snippets

(1) JERRY'S MOTEL AT 3RD & LUCAS:
   "Hey, they have ESPN:" Fish
   "I'm at the top of a hill. I can look down on the City:" Bonds
(2) It is raining: Fish puts a wash basin on his head. It is easy to love Don Quixote.
(3) Bonds is holding up a cardboard "No Parking" sign at the entrance to the 110 at Bixel.
   Fish comes by: "Hey, isn't that supposed to say 'Will Work for Food?'"

Chapter 54.
MacArthur Park

PIGEONS ARE EATING TORTILLAS AT 7th and Westlake. There are about a dozen pigeons and about a dozen tortillas, so the birds are not fighting. The tortillas are huge so the pigeons are instead struggling to tear away bits of the flat bread while not forsaking the whole piece. Sparrows are darting in and out for the crumbs while avoiding the pigeons' possessive threats.

It is seven AM. Few people are on the streets. Little is open—a small plywood newsstand at Alvarado. Langer's Deli, a hold-over since 1947, does not open until eight. Fish used to love their pastrami.

The sidewalk is black with trampled gum. Paper wrappers and cups of plastic and Styrofoam whirl and eddy in the gutters and doorways. Within two hours, the streets will be full of commerce—legal and illegal, above-board and under-the-table.

Fish and Soap and Bonds are on an excursion, by foot, from Crown Hill to MacArthur Park.

"Why're we going here?" Soap asks.

"You got something better to do?" Fish asks defiantly in return.

"That ain't no answer," Bonds says.

"OK. I want to see the fountains," Fish says. "You know, someone left the cake out in the rain."

"Yeah, that's right, it says 'RAIN;' it don't say nothing about no fountains." Bonds is armed with his arguing voice and his fighting words.

"What are you saying, there ain't no fountains? There's fountains."

"Stew says 'crack…'"

"What? Who the fuck is Stew?"

"Never mind…"

"What? You fucking with me now?"

"Cool down," Bonds says. He got what he wanted—a rise out of Fish, who always had plans, who wore them all out traipsing around the city, but shit, he was right; at least it was something to do. Bonds smiles to himself, but continues anyway. "What the fuck we arguing for anyway? Who gives a rat shit about fucking fountains?"

Fish, still a bit hot and bothered: "I do. OK?"

"Shit," Bonds chuckles.

"You guys," Soap says. "You argue about everything."

"So Soap, you're along for the ride. Whatta you coming here for? You could be down gettin' vegetables for soup, eatin' soup, drinkin' your damn food or smokin'. We should call you 'Soup…'"

"Now, now," Bonds says.

"You don't have to stick up for me. I came for a hotdog," Soap says. "I want to get a fucking hotdog."

"I don't want shit," Bonds says. "I came here 'cause of you." He pauses for effect. "And because I ain't got nothing better to do…"

They all laugh.

Soap: "I saw Rosie O'Donnell on the TV at the clinic the other day. She says Melanie Griffith puts 'fucking' in the middle of words."

Bonds: "Who's Rosie O'Donnell?"

Fish, at the same time: "Whatta ya mean?"

"She's an actress, I saw her on some talk show. Anyway, Melanie Griffith says, 'hot fucking dog.'"

"Me, too," Bonds says. "I say hot fucking dog. I'm with Soap, 'cept I don't want a hot dog; I want a 'hot fucking dog'."

They laugh some more.

Like the streets, the park is empty at seven, full by nine.

By ten o'clock varied throngs billow in all niches of the space: peddlers and protesters, panhandlers, dope dealers and wanderers.

The trio visits each nook and cranny.

"Weed? Meth? Coke?"

Bonds: "I 'just say no.'"

"Empanadas? Pupusas? Dos por un dolar!"

"What?" Fish asks. "What are they selling?"

Soap: "It don't matter. We can't afford it anyway."

"Hey, it may be cheaper than a hot fucking dog…"

"Yeah, but what the fuck is it?" Fish asks again.

"I wish I spoke Spanish," Soap says. "Everybody else does."

A party for a kid, a girl, fifteen, a quinceñera. Though the trio does not know the word, or the importance of the girl's coming out, they know the number: 15—in big letters and small, on banners, on signs, on balloons—with Selena on the boom box, frilly dresses, beer and Penafiel, the party Friday, not Saturday or Sunday because the parents work, cleaning rooms and dishes at hotels downtown, all weekend.

"Fifteen must be their lucky number," Fish says.

"I wish I spoke Spanish," Soap says again.

"Will you stop saying that..."

On a bench, four or five men strumming guitars and other stringed instruments—mariachis practicing for a wedding they'll play tomorrow; on another bench, two or three men drinking Gallo Port, but speaking Spanish.

The men smile at Soap—and at Fish and at Bonds, too. Bonds nods at them, gravely almost, but with respect. Fish is suspicious of the motives of their smiles. He does not acknowledge them. The men laugh. Fish is about to open his mouth, but Bonds stops him wordlessly, putting a hand to his shoulder. Soap and Bonds are both glad for the contact, however fleeting and thin. But they can't talk with the men either, and they do not stop.

A rally of La Raza is assembling at the northwest end of the park. Campaign workers are putting up a small, makeshift stage. They are hanging banners in red, white and blue, as well as rafts of Mexican flags. Very young men and women in dress clothes are testing microphones with the standard "test: one, two, three; test: one, two, three..., but then in Spanish, too—"listo; uno, dos, tres..." A truck pulls up and a crew sets up tables and chairs—long, folding tables, some bedecked with flyers, others with hot trays for food.

"Hey, Soap," Bonds says, pointing at the gathering. "You may get your fucking hot dog after all."

"That's hot fucking dog."

"Yes, yes, Melanie. I'm sorry: hot fucking dog."

"Let's go check it out," Fish says.

A gaggle of even younger men and women are gathered around a short, stout Latino man, wearing a tie at half-mast and shouting into a megaphone:

"Our goal is to register 10,000 people this week. We have to defeat this evil measure. We can't let Pete Wilson get away with destroying all that America stands for."

He is practicing his speech.

The crowd of young people are all carrying clip boards.

Fish and Soap and Bonds take seats in the grass at the fringes of the rally area.

"Let's see what kind of food they bring," Fish says, sitting down heavily.

"You got money?" Bonds asks.

"It'll be free," Soap says.

Bonds: "Bullshit. You'll have to make some kind of donation or some shit."

Soap says, "A couple years ago, Winchell's gave free donuts if you voted."

"Did you vote?" Fish asks.

"No. I didn't know where to vote at..."

"Exactly. You can't just walk up and vote. You gotta register; you gotta have a place to live, an address and shit. It don't happen just like that." Fish snaps his fingers. "Shit, I can't remember the last time I voted."

"I remember voting for a guy named Floyd James for Compton City Council. Then he got his ass thrown in jail."

"Yeah?"

"Yeah. That's when I had the restaurant..." Bonds voice trails off.

"Well, let's wait and see. I bet this shit's going to be free..."

"Nothing's free," Bonds adds as a tag line.

Within a half hour, the rally gets going. Fish and Soap and Bonds listen to speeches—some in English, some in Spanish. When the food comes, they get in a long line—not at the front, so as not to appear too eager or too noticeable, but not at the back of the line either, right smack in the middle. There are plates of beans and rice, tamales and taquitos, though only Bonds knows what taquitos and tamales are. The other two look warily at some of the Mexican food, but ask no questions. A little further down in the line, a crush of kids crunch up, jumping and climbing over one another like NBA players positioning for a rebound.

"Hey, Soap, look: hot fucking dogs," Bonds shouts.

A half dozen adults swivel and stare their disapproval at the loudly spoken cuss word.

"So much for not being noticed," Fish says. "Let's go."

Soap: "That's all you ever say, 'let's go; let's go' I want a hot effin' dog..."

"They're going to throw us out."

Bonds: "What do you mean throw us out. This is a public park."

"Well, let's go over to the public part, OK— with those guys like us, drinking Night Train..."

"Port, it was Port..."

"Whatever, let's go."

In the middle of the argument, a young Latino in a pony tail approaches them.

"Está bien," he says. "I mean, it's OK. Are you guys registered to vote?"

"We don't live around here." Bonds says.

"You live in LA County?"

"We move around a lot," Soap says.

"Look, don't mean to put you on the spot, but if you got a place where you can pick up mail, any kind of address, you can register to vote. You got a right to vote."

Fish: "Are you saying we're bums?"

Bonds, with some excitement in his voice: "It's awright. He got a point. How we do this?"

"Just fill this form out, and they'll send voter information to wherever you get your mail."

Fish: "Hey, what's this about anyway."

"They're going to put something on the ballot saying immigrants shouldn't be able to go to school or get health care. Pregnant mothers couldn't go to the doctor…"

"That ain't right," Soap says.

"Immigrant, poor, black, brown, white; it don't matter. If you're at the bottom of the barrel, they're gonna try to keep you there," Fish adds.

"That's for sure," the young activist says.

"Sign us up," Bonds says.

They all three register, and when they are done, they quickly grab their food—both Mexican food and hot dogs—and go back to their seats in the grass.

Fish: "I didn't know you was such a politician…"

"I used to be active in Compton—city council, school board elections, shit like that."

"Yeah?"

"You know that guy Floyd James I was telling you about? I didn't just vote for him. I worked on his campaign. Then he does some stupid shit, gets thrown in jail, I get disgusted. Then I lose the restaurant, I get more disgusted; that's the end of that shit…for me anyway…"

"You seemed pretty excited talking to that guy," Soap says.

The speeches get louder.

Bonds gestures towards the makeshift stage: "This stirs up some memories."

"Vote or not, it don't seem to make no difference," Fish says.

"That's because we don't have no power. We don't stick together."

Fish takes out a bottle of Wild Irish Rose that he has been saving for just the proper occasion. He opens it up and passes it around.

"What's with you and this Irish Rose shit?" Bonds asks.

"You got something against the Irish? You don't like my wine? Then fine, more for me and Soap…"

"Don't get touchy."

"Shit, what you got? Next time, bring some Night Train, you like that shit so much."

"Will you guys shut up and pass the booze," Soap says.

The crowd has grown considerably and the speaker now is hitting all the notes. His voice is strong, his pace has rhythm, his words sound powerful. But he is speaking Spanish.

"Sounds like a Baptist preacher...." Bonds says.

"I wish I spoke Spanish," Soap says.

"I agree, girl. I agree."

They pass the bottle around and its contents quickly disappear. They fall asleep on the grass.

When they wake up all that remains of the rally is a bit of errant trash, a few scattered leaflets, a forgotten banner: Vota Ahora, Vota Ahora.

They brush grass and dust off themselves, rub afternoon sleep from their eyes, and begin their walk in silence back to Crown Hill.

Chapter 55.
Liminal

THE PURPLE FLOWERS OF THE jacanranda lay down on Lucas Street like royal carpet. It is a warm spring day. New birds have hatched and the trees scattered among the vacant lots are aflutter with movement and pregnant with noise.

Fish and Soap and Bonds are throwing sticks to a stray dog that has joined them temporarily.

A soccer game is fast and frenetic at the Belmont Tunnel, the City's first and long-abandoned attempt at a subway. The walls there are covered with graffiti, the script bright not ominous this time.

The dog is having fun.

So far, so good…

Chapter 56.
Bonds
"Water"

RAIN POURING. DRENCHED, DEPRESSED. COUGH and cold: no way to go away.
Soaked through. All days the same, Monday, Tuesday, Wednesday, no matter.
Fish knows this shit; I don't. He reads the paper. Just know. Know only—can't
remember: last day I was dry. Rain still. Seems—rain always. For now anyway.
Now and how long. How long? Not long. Not long? Too long. That I know.
Fucking wet, not dry. Always wet. For now. Months maybe. Weeks anyway.
Shit.

Fish
"Fire"

I have never lit a fire in a trash can.

Soap
"Air"

It's all out of order now, floating like a crowd. Floating. Floating like a lost
balloon. Floating...

Chapter 57.
Go, Juice, Go

O.J'S IN THE BRONCO.

Who the fuck has ever heard of a slow-speed chase?

The papers say his ex-wife's head was nearly severed.

Slice and dice in Chicago.

Maybe filming a commercial for Benihana.

Slice and Dice.

Ginzu Knives.

A vegetarian chef.

Root vegetables-tough as nails.

"Hey Bonds, let's go cheer for the Juice."

Fish has a sign.

"GO, JUICE, GO."

Bonds: "Fuck that; that rich motherfucker's guilty as hell."

Fish—trying to help.

Later: "If it don't fit you must acquit."

Fish: "See, the man's innocent."

Bonds: "Bullshit."

Chapter 58.
Bugs

COCKROACHES HAVE LIVED ON EARTH virtually unchanged for more than 350 million years. They are normally tropical insects, but we have obliged a few species by providing warm, moist, food-filled houses for them to infest. Tough, fast, prolific and able to learn to avoid poisons, cockroaches often survive our efforts to eradicate them. Although winged, these oval-flat bodied insects rarely fly. They are not directly implicated in the spread of diseases, but their feces and particles from their bodies cause allergies in many people.

American Cockroach
  2 in.
The American Cockroach with antennae longer than its body is one of our largest roaches. This species is often called the sewer roach.

Oriental Cockroach
  1 3/8 in.
This blackish Asian cockroach has a body slightly more beetlelike than other roaches. It is usually found in basements where it has access to water.

Brown-Banded Cockroach
  5/8 in.
The Brown-Banded Cockroach lives all over the house in odd places, like inside the television. It tends to fly more readily than other species. Its sticky egg cases, which like all cockroach egg cases look like little purses, are sometimes found on walls and other vertical surfaces.

German Cockroach
  5/8 in.
The very common Brown German Cockroach seeks water and warmth so it is often seen in the bathroom. It too likes televisions and other warm appliances, which not only provide warm hiding places but supply snacks in the form of various pastes and coatings used during manufacturing.

(Taken from Peterson's First Guides to Urban Wildlife by Sarah B. Landry. Boston: Houghton Mifflin. 1994)

Chapter 59.
Not Grand Larceny

SOAP REMEMBERED HER MAKE-OVER with fondness and pride. She felt so good, forgetting quickly and thoroughly how, at first, no salesgirl wanted to wait on her, recalling only the flush of exuberance as she left the May Company that day, her eyeliner perfect, her lipstick so well-drawn, her cheeks bright with blush.

How long ago it seemed! The times in between running from place to place, never seeming so rich as then, a lousy hundred bucks, less even, among them. Soap is an honest woman, trustworthy and straight-shooting, but who can resist reliving some of their fondest memories forever? Especially one so simple and within reach.

She couldn't steal the make-over, couldn't compel the staff to pamper her for free, but she could get the half of it, snatch the products, try to remember what she learned, how they told her to apply the blush, to outline the lips first before filling them in with lipstick, the way to brush her lashes just so with the mascara. The items were so small—lip liner, a tube of blush, maybe even a bottle of nail polish—no, her nails were too far gone, bitten and bleeding half the time. Surely she could slip a few things into her purse though—a raggedy purse, but good enough—without anyone noticing.

The streets had been unkind in many ways to Soap, but not particularly to her face. The outdoors had lined and tanned it so it looked not unlike she'd spent her time on a ranch in Montana or the mountains of Colorado—rather than on the streets of Los Angeles. Ah, but with a little make-up! What a difference. Fish would really like it. They needed a good night.

Soap poked around in the bus system and found her way to the Beverly Center. She wanted to go back to the May Company, but not back downtown to 7th Street where she'd gotten her make-over. They might remember her there. She took a bus south on La Cienega and got off at the corner of Beverly. A big billboard announced the mall with the motto: "Don't Blend In." Soap figured she wouldn't have much trouble with that one. She rode the escalator up from La Cienega, and then another escalator and another; she was self-conscious, aware that she did not belong, but no one looked at her—one way or another

The mall was huge, but the May Company was the first big store, just to the left after the bank of escalators. But first Soap stopped at the pet store. She flushed with excitement seeing the dogs and the cats in glass-doored cages.

She cooed at the door of a little Scottish Terrier, tapping at the glass.

"May I help you, ma'am?" a clerk asked, a young man with an unusually British feel about him,

Soap turned, startled.

"Oh," she said.

"Are you interested in this dog?"

"Oh, yes."

"Let me take him out for you and you can hold him." The clerk opened the door and scooped up the dog and handed it to Soap.

She was a little nervous and it showed. She held the dog in a fumbly way.

"Does he have a name?"

"No. That's up to you. And it's a 'she,' so you could call her all sorts of cute little names."

The clerk was very polite, well-mannered for his age, almost decorous in his demeanor.

"She's so cute."

"Yes, she's very sweet and she has a really good disposition. These dogs are great with kids. Do you have children?"

"No, no, I don't…"

Soap cuddled the dog and scratched behind its ears; she put her finger out and the dog nibbled at her bitten nails. She hugged the dog to her chest.

"Do you want her?"

"Oh, yes," Soap said without thinking that the puppy had a price tag.

"She's on sale. Only $400. These dogs are usually $600 or more—pure bred—we have all the papers. You can pay cash or check, or you can use your credit card."

"Oh, well, yes, I like this dog very much," Soap said, recovering, "but I really feel I should get my next dog from the pound. I know they're not pure bred and all, but, you know, if no one claims them after a week or so, I think it's a week," Soap faltering a bit, "you probably know this already, but, you know, they put them to sleep…"

"Yes, ma'am, I understand," the man said, taking the dog from Soap's arms. "That's a very noble thing for you to do."

The clerk seemed a bit haughty now.

"I'm sure this sweet little dog will find a loving home," Soap said. "One with children, I bet."

She turned and rushed out of the store, nearly in tears.

Her eyes damp, she rushed into the May Company. Cosmetics was the first thing, just inside the door, a dozen counters or more—Estee Lauder, Lancome, Clinique, Chanel, Origins—all with their own lines of products. Soap remembered now—facial products, astringents, toners, creams, special soaps; the different kinds of make up—eye liner and eye shadow, lip liner and lipstick, nail polishes, blush, foundation, and powders; then the perfumes—the smells of scores of them filled the air—sprays and the pure kinds you dabbed on in special places, on the wrists and by the ears. There were perfumes with French names, and ones with sexy names, and there were the fragrances named after their designers or movie stars—Tommy Hilfiger and Elizabeth Taylor, Calvin Klein and Carolina Herrera.

Soap could not remember, however, the kind of product they used when she had her make-over. She thought for a minute, but could not recall. Then, in a needless rush, Soap raced for the Clinique counter. Above the counter hung a sign: SPECIAL SALE. Later, Soap could not recall why she was drawn to the products on sale when she was about to steal the items anyway, but she was—inexorably drawn, in fact. Soap was upset, her plan all gone, all awash, run aground back at the pet store, and she acted unsubtle, quickly and rashly. She grabbed items from the counter, not even aware of the contents of the tubes and bottles she tossed almost violently into her purse, her bag, a worn, but large canvas tote with handles. She stared, unseeing, straight at the salesgirl, but the salesgirl saw her and called security immediately. As close as the door was, Soap could not stop loading her bag with cosmetics, let alone make it out of the store. The guards grabbed her and ushered her out back into a windowless cubicle designed specifically for detaining shoplifters.

At her trial, the City Attorney pushed for felony grand larceny. Soap had, he said, willfully and flagrantly stolen more than $200 worth of fine cosmetics from a retail establishment, and furthermore, she was a vagrant. These kinds of aggressive and lawbreaking derelicts intimidate the citizenry and discourage the conduct of legitimate business. The public defender leaned over to Soap, whispering, and assured her that the judge was not nearly so Republican as the eager—in fact, overly eager—young prosecutor.

When it was his turn, the public defender argued eloquently about the indignities of poverty, the trials of being homeless, and the compassion our society should show to those who have fallen through the cracks. Unfortunately, he hardly mentioned Soap by name and barely defended her actions in his statements.

"Poverty might justify the stealing of necessities," the prosecutor argued, "but make up? Top-of-the-line cosmetics at that. Not Maybelline or Revlon from SavOn, but Clinique from the May Company!" His voice soared with poorly-acted outrage.

The judge rolled his eyes. "This is *not* LA Law, Mr. Bart." Then he turned to the PD: "Nor is this a session of Congress debating public policy regarding the poor. Do you have anything to say on behalf of your *client*?"

All at once, Soap remembered the sign: SPECIAL SALE.

She leaned over to her lawyer: "How much does it have to be to be grand larceny?"

"What?"

"You know, how much money does it have to add up to, the stuff I stole? I thought I heard him say there was a limit or something?"

"Yeah, two hundred. But you stole way over that."

"How much?"

The judge: "Counselor, let's hear it."

The public defender to Soap: "More than two hundred dollars worth…"

Soap, interrupting him: "I know. How much more?"

"A lot."

"What's the number? Did they add it up?"

The lawyer looked through some papers. "It's way over."

"How much? How much?"

"Two-hundred-and seventy dollars."

"It was on sale. Did they write down the sale price?"

"How do I know?"

"You're my lawyer."

"I'm not shopping. They don't tell me if stuff's on sale."

"Ask, will you?"

"Why?'

"The stuff was 30% off. How much would that be?"

"Twenty-seven bucks is ten percent. Let's see. Times three, that's $81. Hell, you're right, now you're down to $189."

While the whispered conversation between Soap and her lawyer went on, the judge had become increasingly impatient. He started banging his gavel.

"Let's go, let's go. I've got a half-dozen trials waiting for this one to be over. This isn't a capital case, ladies and gentlemen. Hurry it up."

"I agree, your honor," the prosecutor piped in. "I cannot understand this delay."

"Thanks for your support, but I run this court room, Mr. Bart."

"Your honor, I move to have the charges reduced to misdemeanor simple larceny," the P.D. interjected, "and I ask that the court sentence my client to six months probation for a first offense."

"On what grounds, young man? Your client stole more than $200 worth of merchandise. You're familiar with the statute…"

"Excuse me, your honor, if I'm interrupting, but the items were on sale. I don't believe you can calculate the worth of the merchandise on the basis of its list price, but rather on the price of the items at the time of the theft. My client will agree to plead guilty to a misdemeanor on this basis."

"This is preposterous, your honor," the prosecutor was on his feet again.

"Sit down, Mr. Bart." The judge smiled. "Do we have any way to establish that the items were on sale the day your client stole them?"

"Allegedly, your honor. We haven't agreed to a plea."

"Yes, young man, allegedly. But can you answer my question?"

"I am certain that if you grant us a continuance, we can quickly call the store and look up the records on computer, and bring in a print-out of some sort to the court—perhaps even as soon as tomorrow."

"I'm inclined to agree. My wife goes to those sales all the time. The list price is seldom the final price."

"Your honor…"

"Excuse me, Mr. Bart. I was in the middle of my decision. Counselor, bring me evidence of the sale dates tomorrow. Just file them with the clerk. I'll agree to six months probation in exchange for a guilty plea to petty theft."

The public defender looked at the nodding Soap.

"Agreed, your honor."

"Finally, the judge said. "Case closed." He banged the gavel to preempt Mr. Bart. "Next."

Soap hugged her young lawyer, not knowing she had won him his first case. She went downstairs to sign a few papers and soon was on the streets of West LA, near the 405 Freeway, unfamiliar territory, in search of a bus to Hollywood to find Bonds and Fish—yes, Bonds and Fish, but especially Fish, who would be worried and missing her terribly. Besides, what a great story she had to tell, and—whether they believed it or not—she knew in her heart it was true and she would tell it all over town.

Chapter 60.
At the "Back Door" (II)

"MY SECOND HUSBAND WAS RICH," Soap says. "But he made me sign one of those agreements."

"Pre-nup," Bonds says.

"Yeah."

"Anyway, I didn't even think twice. I mean, he had a boat. We went sailing. He took me all over the place."

"Soap?" Fish says.

"I had my own job," she says.

"I know, I know," Fish says.

"I had his picture," Soap says. "Then the last time I was in the hospital, they took it away. I don't know why."

Bonds is waiting for the next part of the story.

Fish is trying to hang in there; the story is not about him.

"We went to Greece once. I'd never been out of the country. We danced and we broke plates on the floor…" Soap starts to cry and then she stops herself. She is neither maudlin nor self-indulgent. She is strong.

"Fucker stayed in Greece," she says. "With some twenty-year old. I came back to Los Angeles without shit. He had that goddamn agreement…Hey, Bonds, what's it called?"

"A pre-nup."

"Yeah, that's it."

Chapter 61.
Friends: Best of Times

"Man, I see this guy and he's about the worst bum I know. Standing there with this shit-ass cup and not saying a goddamn word, or at least that I can hear. So I says to him, 'What the fuck you think I am? Bill Gates? Michael fucking Eisner? I'm a bum, just like you.'"

"I hate this shit," he says. "O.K., I love it, man—broke and asking asshole motherfuckers for change."

"Shit, I'm thinking I'm telling him to get more outward and shit and they just passed this law on what they call 'aggressive panhandling' like I'm chasing some son-of-a-bitch down the street or some shit, but, shit, what I'm telling this guy turns out to be Fish, my best friend, man, what I'm telling him, get him busted. So I say, hey, fuck this begging shit, you ask to do car windows, at least you're working."

"Then he says, wise-ass, but friendly-like, 'I thought you people didn't do windows.' I mean, I don't get all easy offended anyway, but this cat I know is cool, just cutting up. And I break out laughing like a motherfuckin' hyena. Anyway you know, I was just bullshitting his ass. but fuck it, we go straight out and get some Windex and find a good parking lot and hustle us some window jobs. Artsy neighborhoods are the best, now. The rock and roll guys on Sunset, like Echo Park, they'll give you a buck. Fuck the rich neighborhoods.

"So Fish and me, man, we tight and we got this enterprise and that was the start of this whole thing. Contrary, man, to what you may think, we got it all going on."

Chapter 62.
Catalogue of an Empty Lot

ONE CITY BLOCK. A VACANT peninsula bordered by three streets. Bixel, Emerald, Miramar. Across 3rd Street, the Chamber of Commerce, a school, a street-long empty lot, and small businesses. Above the corner storefront, two stories of apartments. Then a row of three-storey apartment buildings. Just north of 3rd; Jerry's Motel. Cable TV, etc. Down the hill, Bill's Muffler Shop, marked by a large yellow shock absorber hanging at its corner. Greasy, dirty pipes and engine parts lying on the sidewalk. A pink building with a reputation as a whorehouse. Pointing to it, the scepter of a streetlight and wires hanging from a telephone pole: the lot's only intact structure. The lot. The pole alone marks one side. The other two sides half enclosed by a ten-foot fence: part new, part old, chain link fence, chicken wire, coils of barbed wire. Several gates, some small as to single-family houses, others large; all are never closed. The ground is dirt, stained black by grease. Puddles of oil. Shrubbery, weeds. Canvas, wood and tin; cardboard boxes. Encampments. Residents. One dead tree.

Chapter 63.
Addiction

TAKE THE ELEVATOR OR THE escalator, upstairs, it's upstairs; no, that's bad information, it's on the first floor, the young woman behind the counter, wearing a white smock, hair sprayed, hair in place, not moving, make-up perfect, the lines drawn, shapely nails. Then the customers—picking up eyeliner, and perfume, and facial creams and handbags. Soap's got her eyes on it, spies it on the counter, waits, stalks, waits until the salesperson turns her white-smocked back, not looking, no one watching, Soap scoops up the lipstick, puts it in her pocket and begins to run, to run away, heading for the door. Security sees her, gives chase, shouting, "stop her," likely not knowing even what she's done, what she's got, attracted only by her running away. But Soap is gone, she escapes, escapes into the crowd, gets away, gets away with it, with the theft, with stealing the lipstick. Soap stops in the ladies room on the way out of the mall, stops before the mirror, stops breathing so hard, puts some carefully on her lips and smiles.

Chapter 64.
Cans

They won't take my cans anymore. You hear me. They won't buy fucking cans from me. I line up on Alameda like usual, and shit, I know I ain't stayed indoors in a long time—no shower, no shave—and I know I can't take fucking care of myself like I like to, but damn, they won't take my cans. I'm waiting and waiting like always and, when I get to the front, this new guy, some limp dick motherfucker, comes up and says the neighbors are complaining and shit, so I say, "What? What fucking neighbors?"—I mean it's all industrial, or it used to be anyway, so the guy says, "Listen, I'm gonna be frank with you. People around here..." and he points to—I don't know who—waving his finger around and shit, "say we're a magnet for bums—that's their word, not mine, so we're going to be more selective, use more middle men. They'll take your stuff."

"'Fuck,' I said. And then the fucker had the balls to ask me if I understood. Now I gotta sell my cans to a fucking middle man. Instead of five cents, he gives me three. He's a motherfuckin' block away. He got a truck. He waits 'til us poor bastards sell him enough to fill it up, then he drives a fuckin' block. Shit, next week, he'll be in a fuckin' Mercedes truck, the sonuvabitch. It takes me a couple of hours to get a hundred cans, reaching in the garbage, sorting through the trash, walking the soles off my shoes—and, shit, all I used to get—a lousy five bucks. Now it's fuckin' three, and the fucker says he may raise his share. I got no place else to go. I used to make a honest living offa cans."

"Shit," Fish says.

Bonds laughs.

"Well, you know. Like some real money."

"Fuck."

"You know, like ten or twenty bucks."

"Hey, Bonds, when's the last time we were clean enough to get a real job, not cans even, but a real fuckin' job, even for a day?"

Cans, tin cans, aluminum, Coca Cola, Sprite, Diet Coke, Budweiser, Heineken, Peñafiel, Miller. Crushed cans. Kick the can. I'm going to the can. Guinness. Coors. The can-can. Can me. Canned. 7-Up. Orange Crush. Collect the cans. (Why) won't you buy my fucking cans?

Fish, "I made a sign."

Bonds, "What the fuck you talking about?"

Fish takes out a carefully lettered piece of cardboard:

> ## **<u>Text.</u>**

Fish, "Let's try the 110 on-ramp at 8th. Traffic's slow there and when people sit a long time at a light, they feel a little guilty. Sometimes you get a bit more."

Bonds, "You're a smart motherfucker, Fish."

They look at each other for a minute.

Bonds, "What you waiting for—let's go."

Chapter 65.
The Ambassador

BONDS AND FISH WERE DRINKING cheap beer by the edge of the "Field of Dreams," watching young immigrants—from Mexico, from El Salvador, from Guatemala, from other lands—play soccer. It was a hot day, and the mostly small, shirtless bodies were shiny with sweat.

"You know how to play soccer?" Fish asked Bonds.

"No, man, you don't see no Black guys playing soccer."

"Pele was Black."

"Yeah, but he's from Brazil, Fish. Everybody there plays soccer."

"You like the game?"

"I don't know. I don't know much about it. It just looks like a bunch of guys running around..."

"Yeah, they're always moving, but they don't score much so I don't get the point. Just back and forth, run back and forth..."

Each interrupts almost every other sentence the other starts, but neither seems to mind much.

"But it's the sport of the future, man. You got all these guys from South America and Mexico and shit, but now you also got all your suburban kids, used to be in Little League and Pop Warner and shit, now they're all playing soccer. If I had it to do all over again now, forget the restaurant business, man—too flaky, it's always changing—I'd start a soccer store. But, shit, man, I'm having trouble selling recycled cans for three cents, shit..."

"Fuck that, man. We're relaxing now. What was..., I mean, what's your favorite sport? Basketball? ..."

"Yeah, I'm Black so it's got to be basketball..."

"You didn't let me finish. I was making a list: basketball, baseball, football..."

"Football. I love football..."

"Besides, you're the one said all that shit about Black kids and soccer..."

"No, not kids. Like I said all kinds of kids are playing soccer now. I said Black guys, you know, people our age..."

"And I can add hockey and ice skating if you want..."

"What the fuck?..."

"Add to the list..."

"Shit..."

"Of your favorite sports..."

"I said football, Fish. I love football…"

"Tell me about it…" Fish laughs.

"I was…"

"OK, then…"

"You know how I drag you down the Back Door on Monday nights when we have a little dough, and I start yelling and screaming, and none of those are even my team, man. Don't get me wrong, I used to watch everything, all day Sunday, Monday night, games on Holidays, anything on the NFL, man, I never did get into no college football…"

"What's your team?"

"The Raiders, man. But when they were in LA. Now they like us, man, they don't exist, at least not the way they used to…"

"There you go, Bonds, getting all sentimental and shit again. What's the matter with you today?

"I just can't let go of the fact that motherfucker didn't even want to buy cans from me, like I was just riff-raff…"

"You gotta let go of that, man. He's just an asshole. He don't even know you. Some new guy hired to clean up the operation…"

"Yeah, scrap metal, a respectable business. Shit. You know how many stolen cars, fucking drug dealers' cars, cars used in drive-by's and shit are in those piles of crushed heaps. Probably some motherfucking bodies in the trunks, too."

Fish is looking away, lost in other thoughts.

"You ain't even listening to me, man…"

"I got an idea…"

"Oh, shit!"

"Let's stay at the Ambassador tonight…"

"The Ambassador Hotel?"

"Yeah, over on Wilshire…"

"That's been closed for, like, twenty years…"

"I know. That means the cops won't give a shit, then, will they? 'We can check in any time we like…'"

"What?"

"That's a line from an Eagles song…"

"Who?"

"The Eagles…a bunch of white guys with long hair from, like, twenty years ago…"

"Whatever. Fish, I don't know where you get all these fucking crazy ideas…"

"'But you can never leave…'" Fish is mumbling.

"What?"

"That's weird, that's the rest of the line. It goes something like, 'You can check in any time you like, but you can never leave.'"

"Good. See, it's jinxed. We shouldn't go there. End of idea. Let's think of something else to do…"

"Don't tell me you're superstitious?"

"I ain't superstitious. I just don't want to go all the way over to Wilshire Boulevard to some funky-ass place that's been closed for two decades and then find we can't even get on the property 'cause there's shitloads of barbed wire and fucking guard dogs or some shit…"

"Bonds, come on, man."

"Besides you're the one quoting all them creepy song lyrics. The Hawks, the Eagles, whoever the fuck they are, I don't *even* know, and frankly, I don't give a shit."

"No, that's give a damn. 'Frankly, my dear, I don't give a damn.'"

"Aw, fuck. You either had too much beer or not enough. Which is it, man? 'Cause if it's not enough, you can have mine, and just fuck all this crazy shit."

"I'm going to say what I always say: 'You got any better ideas…anything else to do?'"

"You know that's the place Bobby Kennedy got shot?"

"Of course I know that. You think I'm a fucking moron, or something? That's why I want to go there. Catch a little history, maybe get a little dream back…"

Young immigrants, some dressed in club uniforms from Mexico or El Salvador, others in tatters, arrive and leave in droves to play soccer amidst the empty lots and cardboard houses.

"Here we go. Here we fucking go." Bonds sighs. "Where's Soap?"

"We'll find her."

The Ambassador is surrounded by police and by star vans. The gates are open, but lights and cables, cameras and sound booms are scurrying across the deep front lawn, propelled in and out of the open doors of the hotel by scruffy young men and women dressed in jeans and rock band tee-shirts.

"You can't come in."

"We're making a movie."

"About what?"

"The Life and Death of RFK."

Chapter 66.
A Game of Cards

FISH STARTED A CARD GAME, poker, five card draw, and he dealt Bonds in.

The games got intense, played first for cigarettes, then for money, lastly for liquor.

Darkness came and those not playing, including Soap, held flashlights over the make-shift card table.

Fish won game after game. Bonds won none, but everybody knew they were friends. They came together, 'with that soup woman,' to Crown Hill.

"She's good people."
"I don't know about those two with her."
"Nice people usually have nice friends."
"Sometimes you can get mixed up with the wrong crowd."
"What the fuck are we talking about? We're all bums."
"Speak for yourself, asshole."
"I don't trust that Fish guy."
"I don't' trust that Black guy."
"I don't trust either one of them."
"You're just mad 'cause he's winning your boyfriend's money."
"He ain't got any money..."
"Like I say..."
"Just shut up and let them play cards."

Soon Fish had five packs of cigarettes, twenty-nine bucks and seventy-five cents, and six bottles of booze—two Night Train, two bottles of Wild Irish Rose, one Boone's Farm Strawberry Hill, and a bottle of Gallo Port.

After the sixth bottle, things flared up.

One man, called Pug, stood up, pointing at Bonds but looking at Fish, "He's giving you signals."

"I ain't cheating," Fish said truthfully. He had been feeling incredibly lucky.

"You guys are gonna split the loot later on."

Bonds stood up: "I ain't fucking cheating and neither is he."

A noise started in Pug's throat, then stopped abruptly.

"Go ahead. What were you going to call me? Go ahead. Say it. Go ahead.

Call me a nigger."

Fish and the rest of the guys were still sitting down. The spectators had their flashlights trained now on Bonds and Pug.

Pug looked puzzled.

"What? What! What the fuck you talking about?"

Bonds wanted to just hit Pug, but he stopped himself for two reasons. He was much bigger for one, and he didn't get what this whole exchange was about if it wasn't about cheating at cards.

"I said, 'Go ahead and call me nigger.' That's what you were gonna say…"

Another man, Joe, tapped Bonds gently on the shoulder.

"Hey, mister."

Bonds turned around.

"What the fuck you want?"

"Pug is Black."

"Bullshit."

Pug: "What the fuck, you think he's lying. Look at me, man. We're cool here. This is Crown Hill."

Pug started to laugh and Bonds joined in. Pretty soon the whole crowd was full of high-fives, abrazos, and shaking hands. They sat back down to cards and Fish's lucky streak continued, but he blew a few games on purpose, once discarding two aces, just to keep the peace.

Fish and Bonds did everything to forgive and forget, and so did The Crown Hill crowd— except for the jealous, they all loved Soap and wanted her to stay and the others to go—but somehow something had changed. Not because of the fight exactly nor exactly because of the specter and allegations of cheating at cards, but something. It was clear to all three that it was time once again to move on. They spent that night nearby but a world away from Crown Hill, under the 101 at Silver Lake. Fish had an idea for a new home, and he would get up in the middle of the night to scout it out.

Part Three: Hollywood

"Listen to me good 'cause this is all I have for you
Don't matter who you are, this side or that side of the fence
Or you got a pile of money or you can barely pay the rent
When you die and they take you and they put you in the ground
No matter who or what you are—you end up looking brown."
(The Latin Playboys, "Dose.")

Chapter 67.
Drifters

In the stories of life in the outer bay, the starring roles belong to some of the smallest creatures, the ocean's drifters—the plankton. Tremendous in number, myriad plants and animals flow with the currents.

The outer bay is a world of these drifters: one-celled plants, predatory jellies, the larvae of crabs, sea stars and fishes, swarms of copepods and shrimp-like krill. At times the water here teems with billions and billions, floating in shifting clouds.

In their multitude and diversity, they make up vital, complex communities in open waters.

From the spot prawns patrolling the sea floor to the barnacles carpeting rocky tidepools, from the great blue whales plying the ocean's far reaches to the tiny Arctic terns on their pole-to-pole migrations, nearly all life in the ocean owes its being to the [drifters]...

The outer bay's full of tiny drifters: plants and animals too small to see without a microscope.

Some spend their whole lives drifting with the currents. For others, drifting is just a phase...

In open waters, life begins with nourishing pastures of one-celled plants. Where conditions are right—enough light, enough nutrients—marine life flourishes. Where light or nutrients are lacking, the ocean lies as blue and barren as an empty sky.

Conditions are right along the [West] coast, as in few other places, and plant plankton flourish. In spring and summer they color the water a murky golden brown by their sheer numbers.

Hordes of tiny drifting animals graze on the plants. Clouds of copepods, squadrons of gelatinous soft-bodied salps reap the harvest, their populations exploding as they feast on the bounty of these watery pastures.

As these grazers multiply, they spur the growth of voracious predators: darting arrowworms, delicate, but deadly gooseberries and a host of others.

All five live together in a fierce microcosm.
Tiny drifters are the sea's biggest story.

Taken from **The Outer Bay***, Monterey Bay Aquarium, 1996. p 6.*

Chapter 68.
Non-Locality
Spooky Action at a Distance

FISH SICK; FEVER BREAKS; STRETCHES, yawns, feeling better; a new day.

At that exact same moment and instant, in Cheviot Hills, a 78 year old, retired Chevron engineer, wakes, opens his eyes only to draw his last breath.

***

Diminished, but not despoiled

Chapter 69.
Bathrooms

1. Filthy and lacking all supplies
2. Just filthy
3. Dirty, but well stocked
4. Generally clean, but toilet backed up
5. Generally clean, but sink backed up
6. Out of paper towels
7. Out of soap
8. Out of toilet paper
9. Coin-operated
10. For customers only

Chapter 70.
Hollywood, Here We Come

FISH AND SOAP AND BONDS have left Crown Hill for the streets of Hollywood, to join the younger generation, and the old ghosts, on the Boulevard. Unbeknownst to them, or to the runaway kids flocking here, or to the merchants hocking porcelain statuettes of Marilyn and Elvis and James Dean, a Canadian development company is buying up the real estate at the corner of Hollywood and Highland. The plan is to build a permanent home for the Academy Awards. A permanent home. The Roosevelt Hotel has already been renovated, the El Capitan Theater already refurbished. The signs are there, but few suspect the surplus stores, the costume shops will soon be gone. That is still some years away.

When it is early enough, say mid-afternoon, Fish and Soap and Bonds can drink at Snow White's, a funny little cantina just east of Highland, but they agree to leave when the tourists, mostly foreign, thinking of Disneyland, arrive for Happy Hour. The American tourists, like the studios themselves, have long since fled Hollywood for Studio City and Burbank, protected and ensconced, for now at least, until lower labor and production costs chase this industry, like so many others, to other lands. But who knows. It's America in the nineties. Alan Greenspan's in charge and they may succeed in driving wages down so far here in LA that they can stay. Please don't go to the Third World; just wait, and we'll bring it to you. It's 1994 in California. Big business opposes the anti-immigrant measure on the November ballot. For all the wrong reasons. They've brought in the old Cabinet—Kemp and Bennett—to quell the Right. Too bad. It's the guys that make eight bucks an hour that will vote for it. How about giving us all a raise? Fat chance.

One day Bonds forks out the dough for a cheap boom box from a souvenir joint on the south side of the boulevard. Soap wants to buy the porcelain James Dean, but Fish advises against it.

"Where are you going to put it?" he asks.

Soap wants to cry, but holds it back. 'Stay strong,' she tells herself.

"I can carry it around with me," she says.

"It'll break."

Soap puts it back on the shelf.

Fish puts his arm around her. "I'll buy it for you when we get a place."

Soap just looks at him, neither anger nor tenderness in her eyes.

Though she asks no question, Fish replies.

"Soon, honey. Soon."

They leave the shop to some stares they don't understand from tourists they think are speaking French. What do those stares mean? Shame on you; you look like bums? Shame on your country; how can *Les Etats Unis* allow it?

Bonds stares back, thinking about this, then asks Fish, but it comes out just—"What are they staring at?"—and Fish says, simply, "Us."

The trio walks along, listening to Motown oldies on K-EARTH 101 and looking at the stars carefully crafted into the sidewalk.

Fish remembers the Kinks' song, and they see a lot of names they've never heard of. Then, "Hey, there's Buster Keaton."

"Who?"

"You know, I've lived in LA five years and I never been here before," Soap says.

"I been here my whole life and I ain't been here before," Bonds says.

"I told you you'd like living in Hollywood," Fish replies.

It's mid-day and getting hot so they duck into the large doorway of the El Capitan to get some shade. There are no patrons yet. It's too early for the movies.

'Midnight Train to Georgia' comes on the radio and Bonds turns up the volume.

The stereo is cheap and the music comes out loud and distorted, but the three begin to dance and sing. Bonds has a pretty good voice, honed in the church choir, and he takes the lead, trying out a falsetto and then other voices to pay homage to Gladys. Fish and Soap are the Pips, trying to synchronize their twirls to the lines of the chorus: 'He's leaving/ Leaving. Leaving on the midnight train to Georgia/ Leaving on the midnight train. I'd rather live in his world/world/world/ his and his alone/than live without him in mine....'

At the height of their fun, the manager emerges, a small, overly-dapper man full of self-importance.

"Get out of here, you bums," he shouts, without any attempt to be decent.

"Fuck you," Fish shouts and lunges at the man, no arms raised, no fists clenched, but to get in his face and scream, just scream, move all the bile out from the bottom of his gut with loud words—'*where the fuck does that little asshole get off calling us bums...*'

Bonds holds him back.

"It ain't worth it, man. It ain't fucking worth it."

"Get out of here or I'm calling the police," the officious manager continues, recomposed now after Fish's charge, seeing the size of Bonds and knowing Fish is restrained.

"I work for Disney, asshole. We're *investing* in Hollywood, you know. Your kind aren't long for *this* neighborhood. You can just go back to Skid Row where you belong."

Bonds picks up the radio and shepherds Fish and Soap—both visibly upset, Fish still cussing a blue streak, but Bonds calm—east on the Boulevard to friendlier territory, past Las Palmas, east to where the restoration of Hollywood has not reached.

The cheap boom box, made in China, labor costs not a factor in the price, plays clearly now, the volume down, but the song now is a sad song.

Chapter 71.
Sanctuaries and Rituals

Burger King on Highland	Washing up in the morning	"The manager lets us in before they open—every day. No food though."
The doorway of the old Egyptian theater	Eating lunch	"A cheap slice of pizza, seagulled scraps, 49 cent tacos."
Openings at downtown galleries	Free booze	"Most times they chase us out."
The Hollywood Y	Showers	"The only ones we get."
Sunday brunch at the missions	A hearty meal	"Avoid the sermons."
Wednesdays at Saint Ambrose	Free bag lunch	"The lady there is really nice."
Public bathrooms	Basic human functions	op. cit.
On the street in front of Home Depot	Work for a day	"Rip off."

Chapter 72.
Baton

ba·ton (b- tän, ba-) **n.** [Fr. baton < O Fr. baston < VL.* basto, a stick] **1.**
A staff serving as a symbol of office **2.** *A short, narrow, diagonal bend on a*
coat of arms: in England, such a bend placed sinisterly and cut short at both
ends indicated bastardly : cf. BEND SINISTER **3.** *A slender stick used by a*
conductor in directing an orchestra, choir, etc. **4.** *A hollow metal rod, with a*
knob at one end, twirled in a showy way by a drum major or majorette **5.** *The*
short, light rod passed from one runner to the next in a relay race **6.** *[Brit.] A*
policeman's billy; truncheon

Webster's New World Dictionary of the American Language *David B.*
Guralink (ed.) Cleveland, OH: William Collins Publishers, Inc., p. 119.

Chapter 73.
Little Richard

A LIMO DRIVES BY ON Hollywood Boulevard, past the Supply Sergeant and the tattoo studio. A man in the back, a celebrity perhaps, rolls down the window, and is handing out something to the throng rushing to the car. Fish and Soap and Bonds are walking along, laughing and drinking coffee they managed to get from In and Out Burger, but they are on the other side of the street.

"Hey, who's that? Who's that? A star?"

They hurry across the Boulevard.

"Hey, that's Little Richard," Bonds says when they have a clear view.

"I think he calls himself something else now," Fish says.

Bonds: "Fuck that."

"Look, he's passing out autographs," Soap says.

He *is* handing out lots of something, but they cannot see yet just what it is.

"Shit, I want one," Bonds says. "'Good Golly, Miss Molly.'"

He dashes across the street and Little Richard hands him something, a book. It's a book about the Christian way. A book for the street kids in Hollywood. A book about God.

"What does it say?" Fish asks.

"It's like a Bible," Bonds says.

Soap: "It'll be good for us."

Fish: "I think he's a TV preacher now, ain't he?"

Bonds is flipping through the pages, front to back, then back to front, then one at a time.

"He didn't even sign it."

"He's trying to help people." Soap says. "It'll do us some good."

"Damn," Bonds says.

Fish is smiling, but he's not sure why. He's enjoyed the Masses he's gone to lately, first downtown with the immigrants at La Placita, now a few times at Blessed Sacrament, hearing the Jesuits explain the Gospel to him.

"Read it to us, Bonds," Soap says. "Don't forget. You were a fucking deacon…Or, we can read it to each other, you know, like kids…like we take turns…"

Bonds looks to laugh, but he can see she is serious; and, Fish seems studious, staring off, daydreaming. Bonds realizes he feels serious, too.

"Awright," he says. "I will. Awright."

Neither Fish nor Soap say a word.

After a minute of just standing there, silent, Soap gives Bonds a hug. Bonds puts the book in his pocket.

"Let's get some food and find a doorway for later. It's already six o'clock. I'll preach to y'all tonight. I got a flashlight."

On Hollywood Boulevard, the stars are on the sidewalk, not in the sky.

Chapter 74.
Chaos Theory Revisited

INSIDE A NON-DESCRIPT BUILDING downtown, Tawny is practicing. Rod's cock is long, but length is not his chief virtue. It is almost a full foot in circumference. Nearly twelve inches around. Videos starring Rod always sell well. But so far no one has been able to get the whole thing in their month. Jean-Paul thinks Tawny can do it. And he thinks he'll make tons of money if she can. He is watching now but not filming. He will give Tawny a $5000 bonus if she can do it in rehearsal, a shitload more if she can do it on camera. She is eager to try.

Outside a 36-year-old lawyer in a Hickey Freeman suit is hurrying to court. Not looking, pre-occupied with the litigation drama that awaits him, he trips over a cardboard box stretched across the sidewalk. The lawyer scurries along without a pause. The man in the box crawls out to see what rocked him; he fears he is being rousted by the cops. When he steps outside, blinking in the morning sun, he looks this way and that, but sees nobody anywhere nearby. Given that it is morning, he gathers up his blankets and belongings, folds up his box, puts it all in a shopping cart and heads for the Union Rescue Mission.

Three days later, after much gagging and practice, Tawny succeeds in taking all of Rod's cock in her mouth. Jean-Paul is so excited that he has her suck him too before giving her all kinds of money.

After a month-long trial, the lawyer wins his case on behalf of an insurance company. He is sure to make full partner now.

The man in the box spends his time in and out of jail. During the rains his box is ruined. It takes him nearly two weeks to get a hold of a new one.

Chapter 75.
Observations at Snow White's

On the Weather: It takes a long time to make ice, very little time to melt it.

On Booze: "I've worked in high-class bars and in the worst of dives, and I don't care whether it's expensive champagne or cheap beer, all stale booze smells the same in the morning."

On Population: "Reliable estimates say there are nearly six billion of us on this planet now."

From the Bible: *You shall indeed hear, but never understand, and you shall indeed see, but never perceive. Acts 28:26.*

From the Streets: "Too much is just as bad as not enough."

Realus Hill, Ruth's Kitchen
Compton, California

Chapter 76.
Boots

BONDS WOKE UP AFTER THE long night, the good times, the wine, the good cheer, with Fish and Soap and with all his friends, and, as often happened, too much, over-indulgence, the details hazy at best, Bonds tried to think: where the fuck am I now? Where the hell am I waking up? There was light in the room, too much for his aching head. And, shit, he was on a bed, a real bed, mattress, box spring, the whole shebang, not some cardboard box, not the concrete of a thousand alleyways; this was a motherfuckin' bed, goddamn it!! His eyes open now, the peeling paint, his head throbbing, sure, of course; the bare light bulb swaying in a soft breeze, no cover, but politely turned off, someone had cared for him last night; his teeth coated with thick spit, each one covered as with an itchy sweater. Ahhh!!!! Bonds opened his eyes again and again until he could see clearly, grasp the full measure of the scene—a fleabag hotel, but a hotel nonetheless, yes sir. Then he saw, then he remembered; they were by the door, lined up like soldiers, lined up like grave stones, lined up like kindergarten kids at recess—his new shoes, boots, ten holes, laced up front, a gift, a present, yes, he had it now, something fine, something nice, a good deed done to him. He had new shoes, shiny new boots, the only new thing he'd owned in years, and this time, an anchor, something that held him to the ground, something to replace his torn, old tennis shoes, holes and all, Reeboks though they may be, old, stinky motherfuckin' things now, for sure. But no more. Not now. All different now. At last, something new. He'd done it right. Yeah. And, it'd been done right by him. A story now. Something to be told. Something grand. Oh yes. Where was Fish? Where was Soap? A bottle of Night Train? Something to suck on? For he was alone in this hotel room. Yes, alone. Now he would go out into the world, he would find his mates, search for his friends, hunt down his compadres, and tell his story. It would dominate the night. Bonds scored, man. He had the winning ticket. The big enchilada. And, he had the new boots to show for it, to prove it, to face down the charges of "Bullshit!" of disbelief. But he had a ringer. He got the girl and came away with a new pair of boots. Who the fuck was going to beat that one tonight at the Back Door? Who? "I know the answer. Not a single, motherfucker; Nobody, that's who."

Chapter 77.
At the "Back Door" (III)

"MAN, DID I TELL YOU this before? Elmer Dills came to my place, man—Elmer Dills came to fucking Compton," Bonds says.

Of course, they all know the story; of course they say nothing and nod their heads, eager and aware.

"I got this review in the Compton Bulletin—best barbeque in Compton. Like, big fucking deal. I think I was the only fucking barbeque place in god-damn Compton."

"Yeah," Soap says.

"Then I realized that they didn't say just fucking Compton, they said I had the best barbeque in all of South L.A. Fuck Mr. Jim's, fuck Woody's. I was the fucking best."

"Fucking cool," Fish says. "That's fucking great."

"But I have the same business—GM factory at lunch time, shit at night—nothing at all."

Soap rubs Bond's shoulder. "Who the fuck is coming to Compton for dinner? After dark? You got to be fucking kidding me?"

Bonds has some money. He orders another round.

"I knew that shit when I opened up. But fuck it—I wasn't going to go to no Marina fucking del Rey to serve ribs, you know what I mean?"

"I got that," Soap says.

A little crowd is gathering around the table to hear Bonds storytelling.

"Then Elmer fucking Dills walks in the door. Fucking unannounced. I served that muthafucker hot links, ribs, fucking sliced turkey with my special sauce—we cooked the whole fucking bird." Bonds looks around. Everybody is looking at him.

"Fucking Elmer Dills, he eats all this shit, and he looks at me and he says, "I'm going on the air with this. I've never had anything like it."

"So his show runs, like the first of fucking May. They close the GM plant by the middle of the month."

"Well, fuck, ya know I closed up by the fourth of July. Shut down, pad-locks on the fucking door. After that—the goddamn Desert Storm—the fuck-ing Reserves, goddamn gas and shit, every fucking thing."

"Last call," the bartender shouts.

Chapter 78.
Bathroom Report #5

FISH USES A NICE PUBLIC bathroom.

Two businessmen come in. They talk badly about Fish:

"It stinks in here."

"I saw some bum come in here."

"Fucking security. They don't keep anyone out."

Et cetera.

Fish is in a stall. Hears all this. Is meant to.

The two guys go into stalls.

Fish comes out first.

He washes his hands.

On the way out, he turns out the lights.

Men's voices:

"Hey, who turned out the lights?"

"Shit, I can't see to wipe my ass."

"Asshole."

Fish laughs and leaves.

Chapter 79.
Easy Off

I.

I LIKE WATER BECAUSE YOU can spill it. And it never makes a mess. I am homeless so this matters. Sometimes my clothes smell like booze. Sometimes my things are stained. People see this. But with water…Ahhhh!!!! In a minute or an hour, not a sign of it. What do they say? Thank God for small favors…

II.

Of all broken glass, light bulbs are the hardest to sweep up.

Chapter 80.
Story, Interrupted

Fish started to tell his tale, or one of them anyway, the plumbing jobs, the booze, the hole he cut in the wrong guy's wall, how after that mistake, when admittedly he'd been drinking, but just a beer or two at lunch with the boys on the job, they got this work at a hotel, a big one, a new one, where America sleeps away from home, "a motel, hotel, Holiday Inn," and they were working, maybe four o'clock, in any case, the beer all worn off by then for sure, and all of a sudden, out of nowhere, immediately and without a moment's notice, a pipe burst in the wall, a big pipe, down in the basement, in the work rooms, near the water mains, and a monsoon of water, a tsunami, a flash flood came at them straight out, chasing them down the corridor like a lion hunting prey—no faster—a cheetah at top speed, and they ran, ran for their lives and they made it, made it to safety, out of danger, out of harm's way, and when they saw the foremen and the project supervisor, and the VeePee from Holiday Inn, Embassy Suites, he couldn't remember, they thought, the team thought, naively, that number one, they'd be glad to see them alive, not elated, just glad, elated reserved for Fish and his fellow survivors, but management glad there were no deaths, no fatalities, no on the job casualties, but instead of that sentiment, not even an iota of it, the workers were met with blame, with recrimination; they were the scapegoats, someone had to take the rap, the fall, for the failure of those brand new pipes, never mind that it wasn't Fish and his colleagues that had even installed those pipes, that it was the big contractor, the big cheese, the full-service outfit, that had done all the major work, that Fish and his team were just brought in for finish work, for faucets and shower heads, for the details. They were all fired and blacklisted; drinking on the job. They couldn't even volunteer for blood tests. There were too many witnesses to their lunch-time beer drinking, which grew, of course, from modest, to stories of their consuming pitcher after pitcher, loud and raucous, clearly intoxicated, inebriated, under the influence, no matter that it was all bullshit; everyone else's reputations stayed intact, unblemished, blame it on those drunken workers, the ones at the bottom of the food chain, low skilled guys trying to better themselves, yeah, it was their fault, who ever heard of drinking pitchers of beer on a lunch break—high and mighty at the top, the hotel got finished, opened up without a hitch, never a vacancy, no memory of the incident of the flood, or who took the fall.

Fish never got to finish his story. The cops came and chased them out from in front of the Cinerama, shoved them back into the parking lot, in fact, got in their face, pushed them around a bit, no punches, no batons, just sending a message, "this time." So after that, the topic of discussion shifted, Bonds and Fish walking north and west now, the cops gone at last.

"We weren't doing shit/nothing, man."

"Pisses me off."

"They got no fucking right...."

"This is a free country...."

They found a couple of bucks for Night Train and went home to Soap, nestled under the 101.

Chapter 81.
Cheetah's

FISH ALONE: EAST HOLLYWOOD, STARK, streets deserted, like the Mojave, like Death Valley, almost empty, but nocturnal, living things hiding mostly, then out from undercover, brief forays, quick hits, predator and prey. Fish, prey now, alone in the night, walking, four miles, five miles, maybe more—Hollywood Boulevard and Normandie—back to Soap, back to Bonds, back home. Back to Soap especially. Home: under the 101, just at Cahuenga, a long walk now.

Mission accomplished? No. Hardly. Mission failed. Another dream doomed, another hope gone. Quiet as the desert night. Mostly quiet anyway. Urban sounds. Desert sounds. Listen carefully. The loudest place is not in a city. Find a cove in a roiling sea. Listen to the waves slam the rocks, like Sonny Liston's gloves, like Joe Frazier, amplified, over and over, louder than the Hell's Angels' Harleys, louder than Metallica. Back to mission. Under the glow of failure. Another attempt. A shoot and a miss, sure, but better than never trying. Never stop trying. Fish tries to pep talk himself. Always does; often succeeds. There. There's a victory. *Reporter, some time ago, asks me: Are you always sad? I reply: I'm never sad. I'm always happy. No bullshit. Not entirely anyway. Can't let it get you down.*

Fish has dreams.

Heard about a job. This kid, Hollywood kid, nice kid, club on Sunset—the Roxy, the Whiskey, anyway near home, he tells me about a job. The kid's a bartender. Has worked a lot of clubs. They just opened a strip club, Cheetah's, far end of Hollywood Boulevard, closer to our old place in Crown Hill, in fact, but a job's a job. The kid knows the manager, knows they need a maintenance man, after hours, work two to six—in the AM. Clean up, take out the trash, et cetera. Bartender used to close. Wants to leave early. Owner's OK with it. The bartender, he's a favorite with movie stars and hot shots who go to this place, I guess, and the owners, they want a guy they can pay minimum wage to anyways. So I'm the guy. Kid tells me I should go there at closing, at two, talk to the manager then. So I do. I use the kid's name. The guy gives me a beer, free. All the customers are gone. I can see the girls packing up to leave. My eye wanders. They're very nice looking. I didn't tell Soap it was a strip joint. Why start trouble? Like I said before, a job's a job.

The manager's nice, but he levels with me. 'Where you live?' he asks.

'By Cahuenga,' I say.

'You got no place to stay, right?'

'OK, yeah.'

'No way I can hire you.'

'What's that got to do with it.'

'Image.'

'Image? What the fuck are you talking about, this is a strip joint!'

'I know this don't look like shit, but movie stars come in here...'

'So? They ain't gonna be here at three o'clock in the fucking morning when I'm sweeping up in here.'

'The owners would go batshit. You don't know who gets these jobs. Look, if this was Universal Studios, you'd have to be Tom Hanks' kid to be the janitor, OK. Club circuit's the same thing.'

'Shit.'

'They're looking for a young guy, someone hungry, a guy they can promote to bartender if he sticks it out...'

'Don't I look like I could mix a drink?'

'It won't work.'

'You don't know what I can do, what my skills are.'

'I'm telling you, no way. But, I tell you what, I can give you a place to live upstairs. It's got a shower. You can get some temp jobs for a while, save some money, then we'll see what we can do.'

'How big's the place?'

'What are you, picky? It's a fucking glorified closet, but it beats living under the freeway...'

'I ain't gonna get into that, but my question really is: Can the place fit three people?'

'Three people? What the fuck you talking about? You got kids or something?'

'No, but I got a girl, a nice girl, and I got a buddy—he lost his girlfriend—anyway, we go everywhere together...'

'Three people won't fit in there.'

'I can't leave them on the streets.'

'Look, I'm trying to do you a favor. Your connection, Randy, the guy who sent you here, he gave me a call. He said you're a good guy...'

'I know you're trying to help. I ain't mad. But think about it, what do I tell my girl? Hey, I got a place to stay and you don't...'

'Look, I'd be sneaking you in as it is...'

'I understand. Look, if I wanted to bullshit you, I would have said sure, *then snuck my friends in—two, three, ten of them, it don't matter, we don't give a shit how small it is, it's warm…It would have taken you a day or two to find out, throw us out, whatever, but I wouldn't lose shit. I would have split the fuck out of here, a couple days free lodging under my belt, a hero to my friends, and you wouldn't ever've seen me again. I'm an honest man. And it seems you are, too. You feel bad. You want to help. Don't feel bad. You got something to offer me; it ain't much, but it's something. You look at me. You see a desperate man. You think I got to take it. But I can't, you see. I understand you; you only think you understand me. And I don't mean to put you down, and I know you're not meaning to put me down either. So let's just shake hands, I'll say thanks, and you let me get on home…'*

'OK. You're a funny guy. But I do think I understand. You need a ride? I'll be done totaling these receipts in about an hour.'

'That's OK; I got a ride.'

That was the only lie I told.

Fish alone, at night. Stray cats snarling. Night bugs out, moths in the air, beetles on the pavement. Fish is walking faster now, making progress. West of Western already. Not dejected. Still the juices flowing. Diminished, but not despoiled. Almost home.

Chapter 82.
A Friend's Story

"GOT A QUARTER?"

"Spare any change?"

I ask every passerby. Without exception.

I poke my dirty needle—oh, so subtly and swiftly–only into the skin of those who give me money.

Chapter 83.
Public Television

AS USUAL, FISH HAD TROUBLE sleeping, and so he went on a typical early morning expedition—near four or five AM—looking for a newspaper, combing for stories about Rwanda and other issues that touched him, searching for options, searching for peace, while Bonds and Soap slept under the 101.

He ventured far east again, both insomniac and vigorous, always seeming to point back towards downtown and not to Santa Monica and the ocean, always telling himself that one of these mornings he'd try to go to the sea. This time he would walk by Cheetah's again, knowing it was closed, but hoping perhaps to run into the manager working late, to catch a vibe, to land a job. The guy liked him, he thought. Maybe he should have taken that ride he offered. Oh, screw it. Maybe this. Maybe that. If this. If that. Maybe. Maybe.

He wanted not to see: a cop, a whore, a runaway kid, a drug dealer, a pimp, a mugger, a burglar, a cop, especially a cop, but these were people he saw every day, and he mostly liked, so fat chance. But this morning he wasn't in the mood.

He tried to remember what time Tang's Donuts opened. Was it 24 hours or was it 6 AM? He could play some chess. It had been a while, but he thought he'd still be pretty good. Speed chess. He was good with clocks. He started walking faster.

Moving quickly along the south side of Hollywood Boulevard, past Cheetah's—long closed for the night, no sign of the manager, a drunk college boy or two sleeping in cars still parked out front—Fish broke a sweat. After Hollywood becomes Sunset, before Tang's, Fish looked south to north and saw a sign:

> KCET PLEDGE DRIVE
> HELP YOUR PUBLIC TELEVISION STATION
> WE NEED VOLUNTEERS
> GREAT PEOPLE! GREAT FOOD!

Reading the sign, Fish got an idea.

Fish went to their new home under the 101 at Cahuenga, just along Franklin and the Hollywood Hills Café, the "hippest coffee shop in town"—Fish had read it in the paper—to find Soap and Bonds. They were not there. But Fish had ideas where to find them.

He found them fast, Soap up early, Bonds faithfully accompanying her, Soap at 6 AM, Soap at Mann's Chinese, nee Grauman's, nee history LA-style, no one else there yet, no movies for a long time now, long hours elapsing before the first show, the movies shown in the dark, during the dark, after lunch at least—why not at 6 AM?, she thinks—Soap bent over, Bonds watching, Bonds observant, no management, no security, Soap with her feet in Meryl Streep's footprints newly set, in Carole Lombard's, in Marilyn's, in Judy Garland's, so small, and in her handprints, too.

Fish: ready to roll it out, prepared to outline the plan, get them going, hurrying, scurrying, on the move. Beg, borrow, and steal the money to get cleaned up, to bathe, to shower, whichever, to put on the best clothes they got, clean maybe even, and if they're really lucky, very fortunate, if they are charmed, they might buy anew, just a thing or two, a pair of slacks, a shirt a blouse; it all takes money, every option. It all costs.

"Let's go. Gotta go. Let's move it. We got a break. We gotta take it."

Fish slapping Soap's butt as she's bent over Madonna, a recent arrival, a contemporary, her age even and maybe.

Bonds: "Hey, man, what's up?"

"A gourmet meal, bro', that's what."

Fish slapped Soap's ass again, not hard, lovingly in fact, but still, interrupting her reverie in the footprints, so that her response came out angry and fast: "Hey, Fish, cut the shit. Just another one of your harebrained schemes…" she stopped herself there.

Fish hurt at the cut, at the dig, the unexpected snap, Bonds stoic and silent on the side, a slight smile, a smirk perhaps, but more kindly, then, on his lips, "Let's hear it, man," and Soap standing now, an apology in her eyes, facing Fish, all full of attention, and Fish ready to explain.

"I'm up; I'm up; I'm up. OK, Crown Hill was no Crown Jewel. Soap got her watch ripped off, last valuable thing she had, I guess, but this shit's only temporary; we're in Hollywood—we're saving up for some room at the Trylon Hotel, corner of Franklin. Next week, baby, I tell her, next week, won't be no more than next week—"for sure?"—Yeah, baby, it's for sure, sure as shootin', whatever that means. But for now I got us a gig at a TV station. Come on, baby, we're gonna be on TV. Yeah, yeah, we answer some phones, take down some rich peoples' names and credit card numbers and they feed us all we can eat—all we can eat, some of that good shit, too—fancy spaghetti, little tiny shrimp in your salad, shit like that. No, we ain't gonna try and use the credit cards—you get caught doin' that shit; besides Bonds is real good about that moral shit; we ain't gonna rip no one off. Shit, and what kind of guy do you think I am? That was ages ago, Soap. I ain't stealin' nothin'. I got ideas now, baby, plans."

Scruffy but clean, they arrive on foot at the security gate, everyone else in cars.

"We're here to volunteer," Fish said, standing upright, erect, straight, in perfect posture, speaking slowly, enunciating clearly.

"We want to volunteer to raise money for public television," Soap said.

The guard hesitated, halted, wouldn't open the gate right away. The trio were different, not the same, unlike the others. The security guard did not mean to pause, did not intend to; he just did.

"Just open the fucking gate," Bonds tossed into the discussion.

The guard obeyed immediately, heeded the commanding tone in Bonds' voice, did what he was told. The trio walked onto the property.

Inside, in a large open television studio now lined with banks of phones, were gaggles of people dressed in brands, some you could read on the clothing, some you could not tell, but could see were expensive: Polo, DKNY, Guess, Gap, Levi Strauss, Liz Claiborne, Armani, Nautica. Groups of graduate students, young professionals, opera fans, art aficionados. They were standing in clumps like lint.

But before you could get into the great open space filled with food and phones, you had to sign in. Fish hadn't figured on that. A well-coifed, short-haired woman with hip glasses was taking names and matching them to time slots. None of the three of them had a watch. Fish couldn't make up a reservation. He didn't know what time it was, let alone what time to say he'd signed them up for. The lady in front of him, fifty-five maybe, a professor or a professor's wife, had on a small gold wrist watch. Fish could not read it, could not ask Bonds or Soap aloud, or even tell them of their predicament, unbeknownst to them, for fear of being discovered, uncovered, unmasked, thrown out, banished, tossed out on the street— no product for their labor. They'd spent eight dollars getting ready for this and Fish could see Bonds breathing deeply, inhaling the smells of the fine, all-you-can-eat gourmet feast just ahead of them, a sign on an easel: "Tonight's Food Courtesy of: Wolfgang Puck, Joachim Splichal, Fred Eric, Larry Nicola, Michael McCarthy. KCET says 'Thank You.'" Fish had only heard of Wolfgang Puck, but he bet they all were good. Fish knew what to do: he pulled out the only money he had, his lucky quarter, and dropped it on the ground and it rolled, just as he planned, towards the woman's foot. She heard the ping of the coin on the concrete and looked down. Fish was afraid she was going to stoop to pick it up for him. That would ruin it. But, of course, she didn't; she took a step away, in fact. Just right. He'd be damned if he was going to ask the time—too obvious, too close to the prissy woman taking names, too humiliating. He bent down to grab the quarter; his scheme worked; he could see the watch; it was 7:15. The slot must be 7:30, probably an hour of calling. It was their turn. He stepped up to the table.

"Fish Debak, William Bonds and Mary O'Sullivan for 7:30," he said.

"Say your name again, sir." She called him 'sir,' but she was looking them up and down, noticing every stain in the clothes, every hole, every wrinkle.

"Debak, D—E—B—A—K. First name, Thomas. People call me Fish."

"I don't see you on the list, Mr. Debak."

Bonds chuckled.

"I don't see a Bonds or an O'Sullivan either. Are you sure you called to say you were coming."

"Absolutely."

A very tall, very thin man, also wearing glasses, approached.

"We've got some cancellations, Serena," he said.

He looked warmly at all three of them.

Do they have cancellations or is he trying to lend a hand here? Fish wondered.

"I don't see any here," Serena said, looking intently at the list, the sheet of paper, the yes or no, the do or die.

"I'm sure of it," the man said. "Step right in, Mr. Debak. Ms. O'Sullivan. Mr. Bonds."

Fish took Soap's hand, Bonds needed no cue. They all stepped forward.

"It was kind of you to volunteer," the man said. "I'm Roberto. Help yourself to some dinner while you're waiting. There'll be an orientation in about fifteen minutes, and we'll started answering phones around eight. So relax, get some food, see you soon."

Roberto scurried off.

There was a pasta station, a salad station, a sandwich station, and desserts; unlimited soft drinks, but no booze. Coffee courtesy of Starbucks—espresso, cappuccino, macchiato, latte; cream, steamed milk, non-fat, half-and-half—the ultimate choice issue of the 90s.

Fish and Soap and Bonds ate and ate; they packed it in; they pigged out in the best sense—despite the eyes on them, despite the looks, the snobbery, the stares, the grumbling, the whispering, and, again, the eyes, especially the eyes. But they'd made a deal, an agreement, a compact: they were going to have a good time and not let anyone deter them, distract them, knock them off their course. Soap even brought gallon-sized baggies to slip in food-to-go. Roberto formed a halo around their table, protecting them. No one crossed his line. The trio dined in peace.

When the time came for the briefing, Fish and Soap and Bonds were all rapt attention. Bonds was even taking notes on proper phone intake procedures. Roberto came over and bent down, whispering to them, "You don't have to stay. I understand."

Fish replied for the group: "We appreciate what you did for us. We really do. But we really want to help. That part you misunderstand. No offense."

"Ah, OK. Of course," Roberto answered.

"We're not just here for the free food," Bonds added.

Fish poked him in the shoulder.

Soap stayed quiet.

Roberto moved on.

Answering phones, Fish made $425 for the station; Bonds made $650; and, Soap pulled in $875 worth of pledges. She was tops in their one-hour slot, beating out the gourmet coffee drinkers and the brand-name mavens hands-down.

Afterwards, Bonds said he felt they were being watched. He thought the station personnel hovered around them a bit more than they did around the sophisticated set of their dialing for dollars colleagues.

"I think the pricks thought we were gonna run some kind of credit card scam or some shit," he said loudly in the KCET parking lot. "And, Soap makes them the most money. We earned our food. Shit."

"It's OK," Soap said, putting her arm around Bonds' tense shoulder. "We did a good job; we ate really good. It's OK. It really is."

"Motherfuckers don't appreciate it. Shit, man, just add it up. What you raise, Fish—four something? And, me like six and Soap almost nine. Fuck, that's almost two grand. They better feed our butts. Shit."

Soap continued to try to coax peace out of Bonds's shoulders.

Fish threw in an idea: "Hey, fuck it, let's get a beer."

"We spent all our money," Soap said, dropping her comforting hands, dejected now, too, at the thought of their long walk home, penniless and thirsty, desiring a drink.

Fish thought about Cheetah's. Maybe he could ask the manager for a couple of rounds on the house. Shit, no. What was he thinking? Take Soap to a strip joint—where he knows the manager...Even if she was cool, he'd have to explain to both of them his misadventure in the middle of last week's night, his failure, his lack of employment, his non-job, his swing-and-a-miss. No. Not that. Fish thought again.

"Best meal I've had in years," he said. "What was your favorite, Soap? I loved that chicken, you know, the one with the Chinese-tasting sauce. What about you, Bonds? Man, you were eating away at that macaroni salad..."

"Pasta salad, man. They called it pasta salad," Bonds said all serious, then burst out laughing.

Fish and Soap starting laughing, too. And, they started talking about the food.

"Like, it can't be just 'chicken.' It has to be 'Chicken De Vu,' or some shit…"

"'Chicken De Vu,' what the fuck is that; it was some Chinese chicken like I said, like 'Chicken Lo Chow' or some shit."

"No, man," Bonds said. "It was some French name. Shit, I could remember the look of the words from high school…"

"Did you even taste it? I'm telling you, it was Chinese…"

"I don't give a shit what it taste like; I'm just saying the name was French. Like maybe it was Vietnamese or something. The French were in there, you know."

"I know that. Shit. What the fuck you think I am, ignorant?"

"You guys," Soap shouted. "Shut up."

The guard was coming over. They were still in the parking lot.

"We're leaving, we're leaving," Fish said before the guy got even close.

They laughed extra loud now and started for home.

Chapter 84.
Sticks

Walking Stick
Baseball Bat
Match Stick
Baton
Twig
Popsicle Stick
Branch
Cane
Sticks and Stones
Night Stick
Toothpick
Swizzle Stick

Chapter 85.
The Beverly Wilshire

FISH SNUCK INTO THE LOBBY, past the bellhops, past the doormen, past the concierge, looking for all the world like he belonged nowhere within miles of Wilshire and Rodeo. He had twenty dollars clutched in his hand; he squeezed the money so tightly he crumpled it like it was a piece of paper he was about to throw violently away.

Inside he gasped at the plush carpet, the chandeliers, the finery. To his surprise, he drew few looks. He was prepared for stares, snarls, nasty comments, rude remarks. He made his way past a bevy of old women who had just finished lunch, past a group of businessmen in a state he knew well — he could smell the booze on them just walking by. Fish had washed and kind of shaved. Maybe they thought he was a repairman, had come to fix the air conditioners, the washing machines, the dryers, to load the Coke machines, the candy machines, to fill them with cookies and chips and candy and gum. Perhaps they thought he was a janitor, here to sweep up, to mop the floors, to vacuum, to dust, to change the light bulbs. He didn't think he looked like he worked in the restaurant. For one, he was not Latino. (And, he was certainly not the chef...) Second, he wasn't wearing the right clothes; despite his best efforts this morning, he was still pretty dirty — a little grime under his fingernails and all, his face shaven unevenly, done mostly with a sharpened pocketknife, so he looked to have a five o'clock shadow, so fashionable now. Perhaps they thought he was there to fix the elevator, if indeed one was broken; a machine or an appliance of some sort in any case. They clearly believed he worked, labored with his hands; they believed, thought, suspected, took for granted that he had a job at all. Would that they were right, he thought, suddenly his excitement dampened, a touch of melancholy descending on him, but slowly like a package of precious cargo being delivered to a prestigious address.

He snapped quickly from his worries.

Hell, he was going for a drink at the Beverly-Wilshire Hotel!

Maybe he'd meet a pretty woman; certainly he'd never tell Soap, not even that he was there at all, especially after the flap about her makeover. She looked so nice that night...

Scared to ask where to find the bar, Fish wandered through the winding corridors off the lobby. He dipped into the bathroom, elegant and paneled, to piss. His path came to a dead end amidst high-end shops selling items he could not—ever—afford.

"Can I help you, sir?" It was a well-dressed young woman with a name-tag, asking him a question.

"I'm looking for the bar."

"Deliveries are around the back."

Fish smiled brightly. Far from being insulted at her reply, at which he knew he could, and maybe should feel entitled, Fish was satisfied: she thought he worked delivering beer, that he was part of the crew that made the hotel happen, worked not there, but for Budweiser perhaps or Miller or for some other brewery—in any case, a part of the team. Fuck the patrons that could afford the rooms. Fish belonged.

"Thank you," he said.

The woman gave him directions and Fish vanished down the hallway. He believed he would go in the front door, of course.

The place had a nice feel, more comfortable than the hotel, though Fish was still aware how much all this shit must cost: Asian vases, nice wood, expensive fixtures.

Fish took a seat at the bar.

"What kinds of beer do you have?" Fish asked with amazing confidence.

"Bud, Bud Light, Amstel Light, Heineken, Corona, Pilsner Urquell…"

The bartender ran down the names without pause or hesitation. Fish was impressed and he took a long moment to answer.

"Heineken, please." Fish thought his voice was quivering this time, but it wasn't.

The bartender brought the bottle of Heineken, a frosted glass, and a cocktail napkin imprinted with the hotel logo in gold letters. He poured the beer halfway into the glass. Then he rapped his knuckles on the fine wood bar. "OK," he said.

Fish startled at the noise, but the sound intended nothing bad. It was a quirk and a gesture the bartender used all the time, especially with men and new customers, which he meant in a friendly way, a familiar way, to establish a comfort zone, as "OK, buddy" or "Alright, chief" might accomplish in words. He had not worked long at the Beverly Wilshire. Fish jumped back nonetheless.

"Excuse me, sir, do you want to run a tab?"

Fish did not know the price of a beer. He was sure it was not twenty dollars, but he wanted to leave the man a tip, and he wanted to leave with maybe five dollars still in his pocket.

Fish always liked to tip and the guy was nice enough, and besides, there but for the grace of God, you know. In reverse, Fish guessed. A pink slip away. That's what they were saying nowadays in the papers: so many people—"just a paycheck away." Unlike Fish, most never got there. But Fish harbored no ill will—not right now anyhow. Fish thinking, Fish in and out, in and out, lucid now, like most times lately—but still, in and out, in and out, in and out…

"I think I'll be having just the one," Fish spoke carefully.

"Seven dollars," the bartender said.

I can drink two, tip the man two, and still have four bucks leftover. Not bad, Fish thought. I have to tell this story. I'll tell Bonds all about it. No, Bonds will tell Soap. Surely he will. Fuck it. I'll enjoy this alone.

Fish gave the man the crumpled twenty and, without comment, the bartender rang up his bill. He returned with a ten and three ones.

"Thank you, sir."

There were not many people at the bar. It was still early. But an older man in a golf shirt took a seat a few bar stools down from Fish and the bartender went to take his order. The man ordered Scotch—Fish could hear him—and the bartender did the same rapping on the wood with his knuckles when he delivered the drink.

Fish sipped the ice cold Heineken from his perch at the bar and smiled. He was of two minds. He wanted to chug the beer down quickly. He had several reasons: he had been nervous coming here; the beer was perfectly cold now; it was a hot day for autumn; he was thirsty. On the other hand, he wanted to prolong the experience. That was really the only reason to drink slowly, but it was a powerful one. Fish decided on small sips. And he stuck to his plan.

He looked at his money on the bar. He knew it would seem odd if he scooped it all up and stuffed it back in his pocket, but he couldn't take his eyes off it. The classy thing to do is leave it there, only take it when you are ready to go. But what if I get distracted; start paying attention to the sports show on the television, and someone steals it. Oh, fuck it. I came here to enjoy this—once in a lifetime, you know. Maybe Julia Roberts sat here.

Fish finished his beer, considered ordering another one, but he was done. He'd told the bartender he'd only be having one, and besides, he'd done what he'd come to do. He left the man with two bucks tip on just the one beer, stuffed eleven dollars in his pocket and headed back to Hollywood. He could get Soap something with that money, but not here.

Chapter 86.
Baton #2

Officers using motorized equipment while on-duty shall carry their batons in a manner authorized by their commanding officer. The carrying of the baton by officers assigned to intersection traffic control shall be at the option of their commanding officer.

1994/1995
Manual of the Los Angeles Police Department

Chapter 87.
Mugged

THE GUY MEANT WELL, I'M sure, but—as they say—the road to hell is paved with good intentions. I mean, it's getting cold, it's almost November. You know, how here in LA, the cold comes around the time of Halloween—cold as a witch's tit, like they say. So I'm on a not-too-hot part of Highland, pardon the pun, and this guy sees me shivering, and he comes over to me; I never ask him shit, you know what I mean. Excuse me, officer. Pardon my language. I'm reporting a crime that happened to me and I'm a little upset. Well, you know, I'm just south of Santa Monica, I mean I don't know what I'm doing there, I'm just wandering. I'm in a shit-ass mood. I had a little argument with my friend. Well, there's three of us that kind of stick together. No, we don't have a regular address. But we registered to vote and we have a mailing address. I mean if you send a copy of the crime report to me, I can pick it up there and all. Yes, sir, I am trying to be respectful. I don't have much money, but if I get robbed, I think it's still a crime.

Shit…Excuse me again. Are you going to take notes, or something? Yes, the money I lost, excuse me, the money that was robbed from my ass, from me, from my person, was a gift. Does that matter? If you let me tell the story, I can give you a full report, a detailed description of the suspect, etc. Yes, I know it's your job to call a man a suspect or not, but I can tell you exactly what he looks like…Yes, I am a big guy, but this fucker—I mean this guy—you know, I've seen him around—he's crazy. Yeah, we sorta know each other. We live on the streets, man. You kind of get to know who's who. I don't understand why that matters. This motherfucker….OK, officer, I'll try to control my mouth…this guy pulled a knife on me. From behind, yeah. He's a little shit… about five-four. Yes, sir. Again, I'm sorry. Anyway, he came up behind me. I was all jubilant and shit about the 20 bucks. Yes, he put a knife to my throat. Otherwise I would have kicked his motherfuckin' ass. Pardon me. Yeah, I want him arrested. Shit. He took my money. Twenty bucks is enough for a room. I mean, I was going to see if my buddies made any money today, and then we'd split a place. Yeah. Sometimes the Trylon Hotel. Yeah, it's on Franklin. Near Cahuenga, right. Yeah, well I mean it gets rowdy there sometimes, but it's close and fairly clean. Officer, are you implying that I start trouble there? No, sir. You can check with the manager. I mean I may have a drink or two before going to sleep, but that's with my friends, in the privacy of a room I paid for.

Anyway, the man that gave me the money....Yes, sir, a white man. No, I do not know if he was a drug dealer. I mean, I have no reason to suspect that...he did not offer to sell me anything, nothing at all. Yes, I suppose you could say that he could tell from my appearance that I do not have a lot of money to spend. But, excuse me, officer, but what's the point here? It seems to me that if I have money stolen from me, it's the same thing as if they steal it from Michael Jordan. I mean, he's got more to spare. No, officer, I meant no disrespect to his father. I know he was robbed and killed. I wasn't thinking of that. I'm a fan of Michael Jordan's, too. That's nice that your son has his sneakers. My point is that the guy that gave me the money was real flashy about it, made a big deal of it, like he was showing off. I mean there was no one else around...No, not that I could see. The man who robbed me? I guess he came out from a dark parking lot or alley or something. You know that stretch. No, I am not ungrateful that the man gave me 20 dollars. Yes, the first man. I just mean that, maybe by call-ing attention to the fact that he was handing me money...yeah, he was all extra loud and shit...yeah, maybe he was high, I wasn't asking too many questions when I saw the twenty. Anyway, I think the guy that robbed me heard him, you know, the loud voice attracted his attention and that's when he decided to stick me up. Yeah, stick me up. No, he did not have a gun. Like I said he had a knife. Well, that's what I meant by "stick me up." He mugged me, yes. For my 20 dol-lars, yes. You have enough information? I mean I didn't even describe the guy yet. Well, let me tell you what he looks like. Yes, officer, I will get right to the point. I've been trying to. I mean, with all due respect. Yes, like I said, he was short. About five-four. Right, if he came up in front of me, I probably could have taken him—yes, even with the knife. But, like I said, he came up on me from behind and got the blade right against my throat. No, I guess I didn't hear him. My mind was off someplace, I guess, dreaming about my good fortune. Do I think it was a set-up? What do you mean? I don't see no reason why the first guy would give me money just to have the second guy take it. Well, it's your line of work, but I can't think of no reason. Did you get my name? Bonds, William Bonds. No, that's funny, officer, but not James Bond. And the last name has an "s" at the end, you know, B-O-N-D-S. OK, well you let me know, awright? Yes, of course, I'll press charges. I'm tired of this shit. Get back to me now, will you please, officer. You got my address. Send me a copy of your report and all that shit, OK?...Fuck. I'm talking to myself. Shit, I been talking to myself the whole damn time. Fuck, shit, fuck.

Chapter 88.
Not Working

FISH'S FATHER THOUGHT IT WAS a good idea to take the kids to the movies, and so he did, but when he got there, he had no money, so he snuck them in, the father, too; and the usher saw them, he thought, but didn't say anything—everybody knew about the layoffs. Martha thought the movies were too violent and a waste of money, so she didn't come, and in fact, didn't like him to take the boys; thought they were too young, but he liked Clint Eastwood, and so did they, so they saw a "Dirty Harry" picture. It was a first release. They got to cheer together awhile when Harry shot the villain, so they felt better for a short time. On the way home, still in the afternoon, he stopped for a quick beer, the boys waiting outside, patient because they liked the movie, bouncing a ball, and then, after a time, their father came back outside, squinting because it was dark inside the tavern and bright outside. He was not drunk; one at a time on the tab is what he put, only owed the bartender about six bucks. He told the boys that because he had not bought them any popcorn and thought they might be wondering. The semi-pro league was playing ball, and on the way home, they stopped at the field to watch a couple of innings; one of the guys, the catcher, was old, over forty now, but he used to play in the big leagues and he, most times, hit a home run every game in this league. They were not disappointed. He put one clear over the fence, almost into the parking lot of the shopping mall just across the street, a few discount stores. When they passed the hat, the father put in a dollar; it was nearly all he had, but the home run had been worth it. They started for home, the sun just starting to go down, no traffic, quiet on the boulevard. He wanted to stop at another place for a beer, but resisted, the lighted Bud advertisement blinking in the window just as he passed; his friend Joe worked there and would surely give him one on the house; next time, he thought. The kids wanted pizza from the place where the teenagers hung out listening to the jukebox—big, flat pizzas with thin crusts and a good selection of soda, but he had to tell them no; anyway Martha would be cooking. The boys didn't whine about it, but walked on. He stopped in the church to light a candle, worried about his mother's health, and the boys prayed for their grandmother, noticing the tear just inside their father's eye, not coming out, and they assumed she was dying, but they didn't ask. They crossed themselves with holy water on the way out.

When they got home there was Rice-A-Roni on the stove and the boys complained a little because they had it last night, but their parents figured they didn't understand about budgets, so they didn't explain. There was little good on TV, only repeats in the summer so they didn't watch, not even any good cop shows they wouldn't mind seeing twice, so they played with toy soldiers, playing together pretty well for brothers, whining a little again when they couldn't go to sleep at a friend's house who called too late and whose parents said they'd take them all to an amusement park in the morning, but there wasn't enough money for that and they couldn't very well ask the other boy's parents to pay. There were no questions about why Daddy didn't go to work anymore; they liked having him around. Anyway he wouldn't have known what to tell them and neither did she, although she was starting to get angry, but really didn't deep-down blame him, so couldn't and didn't tell him how she felt. The bickering crept up on them slowly like a fire that's hard to start. She got so she put the want ads at his place at the breakfast table in the morning, and put the rest of the paper somewhere else, in the bathroom even, to hide it, but he'd put the ads aside and ask for the sports page, so even though she said nothing, she stomped her feet when she walked and banged the dishes in the sink loudly to let him know she didn't approve, which he ignored and ignored her, but remained good to the boys, taking them with their baseballs to the park, and stopping only occasionally for a beer with the guys on the way home, which the boys didn't mind and didn't tell their mother, even though they knew the tab was now over twenty dollars because he told them, having to tell someone.

One day, the city work crews came to cut down the trees that had stood and swayed on the street since their father had bought the house, still single, some twenty years before, and before the boys were born, long before. He got mad and started yelling at the workers, and they yelled back, and he yelled some more, and then he went outside to pick a fight, grabbing their tools and still yelling. Then the police came to break it up, and he was mad at Martha because she had called the police, wanting to avoid real trouble, to stop it just it time before it got out of hand. Fish and his brother were mad at Martha, too, because she had kept them inside and out of trouble when they had wanted to go outside and help their father fight, but they got over it soon enough and despite their lack of money, all went out for hamburgers, got away from the noise of the saws.

The good days seemed to stop suddenly like a train, and they stopped going to the park to play ball, while he sat on the couch, watching television, and Martha, their mother, got louder about cooking and doing dishes to the point of breaking some plates, and he'd yell, and she'd yell, and the boys tried to pretend they didn't hear her, disappointed.

When finally they moved from that house and away from that neighborhood, he didn't come with them, but didn't stay either, and went someplace else. The boys started asking questions, of her, not of him, and she couldn't answer them, distraught, but he was gone and they weren't, and they didn't like the new place. The silence was useless and unprotective. They didn't like the new guy she let live with them, but didn't say anything, not being accustomed to it, and she either, and they grew up, became teenagers, still playing baseball, played on their high school team that won a cross-town championship, always two years apart and getting older, seeing their father most weekends. He didn't seem so depressed as at first, working now again, still seeing him even after the home run hitter retired, nearly fifty, from the semi-pro league. All the changes inarticulate as rust.

Chapter 89.
"A Night in Hollywood"

Time: 11:06 PM   Citation: "Aggressive Panhandling" Fine: $500.00
                                  Penal Code # 647C

Time: 11:09 PM   Citation: "Loitering"   Fine: *Anger*
                                  Penal Code # 647H

Time: 11:12 PM   Citation: "Littering"   Fine: *Hopelessness*
                                  Vehicle Code # 23112A

Time: 11:17 PM   Citation: "Jaywalking"   Fine: *Indignity*
                                  Vehicle Code # 21955

ACTION:

Fish is on Cahuenga, south of the 101. He asks a man for money. An LAPD officer comes between them.

"Is he bothering you?"

"No, everything's fine, officer."

The cop writes Fish a ticket.

"What's this for?"

"Aggressive panhandling is illegal."

"He wasn't bothering me."

"I didn't ask you."

Fish mutters, but takes the ticket and puts it in his pocket.

"You can't just stand here. Move along."

"I'm not doing anything."

"That's the point."

The cop writes another ticket and hands it to Fish.

"What's this for?"

"Loitering. Now move along."

Fish has a shopping cart full of stuff with him and also a box. They all had moved out of the Trylon earlier in the day. He takes the cart across the street, but leaves the box.

When he gets back across the street, the cop hands him another ticket.

"What the fuck is this one for?"

"Watch your language! Littering. You left that box here. It's litter and you get a ticket for littering."

Fish picks up the box and stomps across the street, not waiting for the light to change. The cop shouts and comes after him. Fish waits, fuming, but restraining himself.

"What now?"

"Jaywalking. Have a nice night."

Chapter 90.
Wilson and Prop. 187 Win

Wednesday, November 9, 1994
Home Edition Section: PART A Page: A-1
By: BILL STALL and CATHLEEN DECKER
TIMES POLITICAL WRITERS

Republican Gov. Pete Wilson rolled to a landslide victory over Democratic challenger Kathleen Brown on Tuesday to complete one of the most dramatic comebacks in California political history, one that thrust him firmly into the ranks of possible Republican contenders for the White House in 1996.

Wilson, 61, rode to a second four-year term on a tide of voter frustration, coupled with anger over crime and illegal immigration....Also sweeping to victory Tuesday was Proposition 187, the emotion-sparking ballot initiative that cuts off free social benefits and education to illegal immigrants. Wilson and other Republicans had made Proposition 187 the centerpiece of their campaigns down the final stretch in October.

Wilson seemed to make a particular effort in his speech to calm tensions spilling over from the emotional campaign over Proposition 187. "What people need to understand is that this issue was never about race or racism," he said. "To the contrary, Californians of every race and color and creed voted not just to send a message, but they voted for fairness and for the rule of law...

This nation-state is a state of legal immigrants, and proud of it." Wilson's campaign was a textbook effort—a text written by Wilson and his longtime team of political advisers over eight successful general election campaigns. They selected three major themes and stuck with them throughout the long election season—crime, illegal immigration and the economy.

More specifically, Wilson rode the "three strikes" prison sentencing issue through the first half of 1994 and then focused on his support of Proposition 187....By November, the opinion polls indicated that a majority of Californians preferred Wilson's positions on crime, the economy and immigration—just as they had all along.

Chapter 91.
Time

TIME CUTS STREET CORNER LIGHT. Vast trash, fields of ripe weeds. Never more, never less. Asking thoughts. Play it one more time; over, done, finished, not complete. Never whole. Nothing unhealthy, typical kid really. Beer and imagination. Same needs, same desires. Clouds piss rain, wet, soaked through. Prefer dry, drought, rainless, cloudless, waterless, land of sunshine. Lawns turn brown—so what? Frozen litter pockmarked in piles—beer cans, cigarette butts, the bags of endless snack foods—Fritos, Lay's, Ruffles, Doritos— boomboxes blasting. A car drives by. Soot and a smile. Unharmed. De-homed. "Last known residence."

Chapter 92.
Penultimate

<small>BACK AT THE EL CAPITAN</small>

Out of money, out of luck, fucked. No damn good. In the ears: the words of Rev. Weeks, "The Lord giveth and the Lord taketh away." Shit; God giveth and the assholes taketh away. Goddamn. Funny. No thought, none at all, nothing about Rev. Weeks, not in twenty years. Not until now. Las Palabras now on Central Avenue. Iglesia Bautista de Jesus Cristo. New rider—he still gotta be there, got to. No. No. No! No! No memories. Fuck! Fuck that. Can't let myself go nowhere near there. Money. Money? Money! Shit, there's more where that came from—straight off. Forget it. Forget. Fuck it. Banish the thought. Toss that shit. Banish the fucking thought...(funny how it sounds—"banish the fucking thought.") Hell, I can understand "never forget." It's just that for me and mine, it's "never remember." Toss that shit. Yeah, that's it, it's far away now, gone, almost gone, far away, real far, very fucking far, yeah...that's what this shit's good for...Night Train, Gallo Port, who gives a fuck...make it go away. Remember nothing. That's right, a little more, a little more nothing. Nada. Nothing. Empty. Deep Empty. Gone. All gone. All the way gone. Fuck off. Fuck that. Forget that shit. Motherfucker. Motherfucker! I can kick your ass. Go away. Get the fuck out of here! Going, going, gone. That's right, gone. Gone! Fucking gone.

Avoid the rest. Avoid the wind. Avoid the rain. Avoid the cold. Doorways, shelter from the storm. Entryways, long deep entryways. O Captain, my Captain! Songs of ourselves. We sing of nowhere, nowhere to go, no place like home. No place to call home. No home. Without a home. Homeless. Home. Less. Home/less.

In the doorway of the El Capitan, once again, perhaps ill-advised, still so, post-harassment, post-yuppie scum, the trio stands. Out of the way, out of the flow, a refuge, a sanctuary—just standing there. Not even the tunes, no stereo, the boombox silent.

It's the middle of the day.

So?

They don't have movies or shows in the middle of the day.

He's the manager.

He won't be in yet.

I bet he will. He's gotta count the money and shit.

Soap, don't worry.

Fish, tell her, we're just gonna hang around the doorway for a while.

What's he gonna do? Yeah, it's cold, it's windy, we need a minute's rest.

He doesn't like us.

Shit, there ain't no place rolls out the welcome mat for us...

Why you scared of this guy anyway?

I don't know. Something about him...

He's just a little fucking wimp.

Yeah, but there is something bad about him.

Yeah, he's an asshole.

No, something else.

Damn, Soap you're scaring me more than that little fucker.

What's this some kind of psychic shit?

I got bad feelings....

'Cause some guy kicked us out of a doorway before.

Shit, how many times we been kicked out of places?

This is different.

What's different?

I don't know.

We're just going to hang out in the doorway of the El Capitan, just for a little while, get out of this wind, warm up a little.

And move on.

No boombox like last time....

You sold the fucking thing....

That's not the plan. We ain't gonna disturb no one, and if that little prick kicks us out we'll leave, we'll just fucking leave, awright?

We're just gonna kick back a minute.

Awright.

Did I tell you I got mugged last night?

Mugged?

Yeah, some guy gives me 20 dollars and this shit ass with a knife comes up and takes it away.

Mugging one of us, shit.

Yeah, pisses me off. I can't remember the last time I had that kind of bank. I mean, like in one shot, man.

How'd he know you had money?

He must of saw the guy give it to me.

Shit.

Yeah, the guy was all extra loud and shit when he gave me the bills.

What'd you do?

Told the fucking cops.

No!

Yeah, I reported the crime, man. Fucks didn't believe me.

Harassed my ass, in fact…

Didn't even see if the motherfucker that robbed me was hiding some place.

Asked me a fucking shit load of questions, like I was fucking stupid.

Pisses me off just to remember it.

Don't get all upset again, Bonds.

No, I mean fuck that, cops treating me like I was the fucking criminal, shit…

Bonds: I was the victim of a crime, man, an innocent fucking victim. They don't give a rat's ass, man. Shit.

It's O.K.

Let me vent, Soap. Get this shit off my chest.

O.K., but you're getting real loud.

Fuck that, man. You worried 'bout that little pussy that works here? I ain't in the mood for his shit, man. He comes out, I'll kick his fucking ass.

Let's take a walk and talk.

I'm comfortable here, Fish. Shit, now you just as nervous as she is.

I just don't want trouble today.

Last I looked, most of the trouble we get in, you fucking start.

Bonds, just 'cause you're in a bad mood, don't take your shit out on me.

You're both shouting now.

Come on, let's go.

Chill out, Soap, we just talking.

Oh, it's you people. I thought I told you to stay away from this property.

Hey Bonds, look it's fuck face again.

Fish, stop it.

You people? Who the fuck you callin' you people, you sniveling, kiss ass motherfucker.

I want you off this property.

Fuck you.

Yeah, what are you going to do, you little shit, kick our ass.

Guys!

The lady could kick your ass.

Some lady!

What'd you say? Say that again, motherfucker.

Are you threatening me?

You bet your ass I'm threatening you, you little prick. I'm gonna kick your ass.

You better crawl back inside, you little fucking rat motherfucker.

I'm calling the police.

Go ahead, you little fuck.

O.K...O.K., see what I mean, let's go.

Soap, don't give me any of that I told you so stuff.

Alright, but let's go.

I'm just getting my shit.

Well, hurry up.

He's calling the cops.

We'll be gone before they get here.

If they get here.

They'll come.

O.K....You there, spread your legs and put your hands up against the wall.

What for? We didn't do nothing.

You're trespassing and the manager here says you hit him.

We didn't do shit.

He wants to press assault charges.

We didn't touch his ass.

Just do what you're told, we'll sort things out later.

Officer, the white man pushed me and shoved me, and the African-American man kicked me from behind.

He's full of shit.

That's a lie.

Continued argument.

Banter

Chatter

Hostility

Violence.

Chapter 93
240.10

In a complex urban society, officers are daily confronted with situations where control must be exercised to effect arrests and to protect the public safety. Control may be achieved through advice, warnings, and persuasion, or by the use of physical force. While the use of reasonable physical force may be necessary in situations which cannot be otherwise controlled, force may not be resorted to unless other reasonable alternatives have been exhausted or would clearly be ineffective under the particular circumstances. Officers are permitted to use whatever force that is reasonable and necessary to protect others and themselves from bodily harm.

1994/1995
Manual of the Los Angles Police Department

Chapter 94.
Baton #3

Fade in:

The baton came down hard and swift and repeatedly, up and down, Bonds shouting, the cops shouting, Soap screaming, Fish silent. It was time. He couldn't just watch. The bright white light of the police car blinding; the flashing red and blue lights spinning in his head; the constant interrupted crackle of the dispatchers—the burglaries, the robberies, the murders to respond to. All the lights and all the booze made the baton freeze in Fish's vision like it was standing still just for a moment, like on the sports shows, in slow motion, 'slo mo,' like under a strobe light at a disco like he had seen on TV. They were aiming blows at Bonds' head, trying to crack his friend's skull. Fish could see red on the night stick that flailed at his friend.

Fish stepped in front of the baton. He felt its thud deep in his brain. Suddenly everything went from slow to fast, staccato, like a Chaplin movie, frenetic and all at once, like it was happening simultaneously. Then nothing distinct, then only pain—intense and continuous, sharp and then dull. Fast events and fading. No sounds, bright light—not outside, inside. Then no sights, no vision. Down, out.

The Disney man was gone.

Bonds and Soap, in tears, were nursing a dying Fish.

"This never happened," the cop's voice trailed off as he and his partner got into their car and sped away.

Fade to black.

Chapter 95.
After the End

THE FIRST AFRICAN BAPTIST CHURCH on Central Avenue was empty save for Soap and Bonds and Reverend Weeks, along with the elderly ladies who came whenever there was a service of any kind, no matter what, and another half dozen usherettes, also senior citizens, clad in white gloves. Graciously, and at his own expense, Reverend Weeks had programs printed: "Homecoming for 'Brother Fish Debak,'" with his dates of birth and death—July 4, 1960 to December 3, 1994—and a picture of Fish that Bonds had carried in his pocket, one that he found after all.

"Where'd the picture come from?" Soap whispered to Bonds. The music had begun. "I had one." Bonds said. "In my wallet. Can't remember where I got it though."

"I never had his picture."

"It's one of them Polaroids. Maybe we were at a Carnival or something."

"It's a little fuzzy."

"Well, you know. Reverend Weeks had to xerox it and shit."

"Bonds."

"What?"

"You're in church."

"Yeah?"

"Don't say 'shit'!"

She didn't mean to repeat the word, it just came out. They both laughed. The usherettes looked at them crossly and they fell silent.

"It's nice, though."

"What?"

"The picture," Soap said, holding it close to her.

"There'll be extra funeral programs." Bonds said, looking around at the near empty sanctuary.

Soap said nothing.

"This will be nice, too."

"What?"

"The service," said Bonds.

"Been a long time since I've been to church."

"Me, too."

"Fish went once, maybe twice."

"Yeah."

"He told me. It was in Spanish."

"You'll like Reverend Weeks. He helps people. Fights for them. Unions, civil rights, you name it."

"Yeah?"

"And, man, can he preach."

"How do you know him?"

"I used to go here. Twenty years. From when I was a kid to when I lost the restaurant…"

"Shuush!" One of the usherettes said.

Reverend Weeks had come to the pulpit. He was dressed in a black suit and purple tie. Some of Fish's friends arrived from downtown, from the Back Door, Barrett and others, and from the bar they hung out at on Hollywood.

The Mourning Committee comforted Soap as a grieving widow.

Reverend Weeks preached a eulogy about a man he did not know, but a man who was a friend to someone he'd known forever, someone he'd seen as a small child in Sunday school, then had lost. Despite not knowing the man, the preacher meant his words of praise with all his heart. He eulogized Fish as a man forgotten, but not forsaken, and he preached about justice. While the pastor's words soared, Bonds remembered his youth, remembered this church, remembered the man in the pulpit, and squeezed Soap's hand.

The Sermon (An Excerpt)

In the midst of the greatest prosperity the world has ever produced, we face some of the gravest and the most grievous wrongs the world has ever seen: Hunger and homelessness made worse because we can end these injustices and we don't. We won't. We ignore injustice. And we abandon our brothers and sisters our fellow children of God. And we do so at our peril, to the danger of us all.

Today, we stand against the icy winds of injustice, clad and comforted in the warm clothing of our convictions, united in our belief that we can warm the hearts of men and women to fight for what is right and fair, decent and just, bonded in our faith that God and history will not allow the Ice Age of inequality to freeze our proud ideals of freedom and equality. So in the words of the Prophet Isaiah. Chapter 25, verses one through five, take out your Holy Books:

"Oh Lord, thou art my God.

I will exalt thee, I will praise thy name for thou hast done wonderful things, plans formed of old, faithful and sure.

For thou hast made the city a heap, the fortified city a ruin; the palace of aliens is a city no more, it will never be rebuilt.

Therefore, strong peoples will glorify thee; cities of ruthless nations will fear thee.

For thou hast been a stronghold to the poor, a stronghold to the needy in his distress, a shelter from the storm and a shade from the heat.

For the blast of the ruthless is like a storm against the wall, like heat in a dry place.

Thou dost subdue the noise of the aliens, as heat by the shade of a cloud, so the song of the ruthless is stilled."

Call and response. The offering, the hymns, the benediction. Amen

Outside, Bonds and Soap greeted the twenty-odd mourners and committee members politely and with gratitude. They had dressed the best they could. Then they were alone.

> Soap looks at Bonds: Let's go.
> Bonds: Where?
> Soap: To the police station….
> Bonds: What?
> Soap: I'm filing a complaint…
> Bonds: About what?
> Soap: Police brutality….
> Bonds: They'll say he assaulted an officer.
> Soap: Let them.
> Bonds: They'll say I assaulted an officer.
> Soap: Let them.
> Bonds: They'll say you assaulted an officer…
> Soap: Let them.
> Bonds: You can't win.
> Soap: So?
> Bonds: Awright, let's go.

Bonds and Soap walk off together.

The streets around the church are now empty. Reverend Weeks drives up in his Lincoln Town Car: "Need a ride…somewhere?"

> Bonds: "No, we're fine…."

They start to walk up Central Avenue toward downtown. It is surely autumn now and the warm, thick air of Los Angeles has turned cool and thin, the sky less brown. The earthquake, the blistering hot summer, fragmented and heavy, the political winds, demonic and cruel, the fires, all bright like destructive celebration, all have passed—for now at least—with the floods still to come. But that is only punctuation, though harsh and forceful as a thunderclap—the big events, the happenings of note and record, without texture and often without connection. By contrast the un-events of daily life, pulled off in chunks or in strips like cotton candy or torn paper, accumulate from top to bottom, leaving our lives so plaintive, so full of longing for what is not, what never is, what never was. Most things turn out badly. Time does not heal all wounds. Things never go away, never. Yet the timelessness of pain should give us hope not despair, yearning not cynicism. We never lack for something to strive for.

Fish is dead; Soap and Bonds go on. They will file a police complaint. Likely to no avail. They will sleep in beds one night out of ten. They will drink; they will laugh and cry and catch colds and get better. They will shiver and they will smile. And so on, back and forth, up and down, non-history, all time.

We know nothing is ever as we dream it will be. But, in the end, nothing is never nothing. It all matters.

About the Author

LARRY FONDATION is the author of the novel *Angry Nights* and the short story collection *Common Criminals*. They are part of a sequence of five books of fiction focusing on the Los Angeles underbelly. The novel *Fish, Soap and Bonds* is the third book. A fourth volume, a collection of short short stories in collaboration with London-based artist, Kate Ruth, is nearly complete.

Fondation has lived in LA since the 1980s and worked for fifteen years as an organizer in South Central Los Angeles, Compton, and East LA. "I think Los Angeles reveals itself most at the margins," Fondation says. "On the street corners, in bars and nightclubs. In the sounds of the traffic, police sirens and helicopters, in the words and music of local bands..."

His fiction and non-fiction have appeared in a range of diverse publications including *Flaunt* (where he is Special Correspondent), *Fiction International*, *Quarterly West*, the *Los Angeles Times* and the *Harvard Business Review*. He has been nominated for a Pushcart Prize.

About the Illustrator

KATE RUTH is an artist who works with many media and in many fields. As a fine artist, Kate both paints and draws. She creates elegant line drawings, often with splashes of color, and her subject matter is as intriguing as her style. Strippers, good-time girls, and denizens of the streets of New York feature prominently in a number of her best-known works. Kate's crisp style and clean lines give all her subjects dignity and beauty. Since 2001, she has published four books of her drawings.

In addition to this work, Kate is a notable stylist and illustrator, with a wide variety of clients, projects and publications. She graduated with Honors in English Literature and Philosophy from Victoria University in 2001.

The Troublesome Amputee Collected Poetry
John Edward Lawson
tpb 1-933293-15-2, $8.95, 104p

From the introduction by Michael Arnzen: "One of the meatiest collections of grizzly, grotey, bizarro poetry you'll ever come across... The stuff that makes you guffaw with laughter and want to read out loud to other unsuspecting people."

Westermead, Scott Thomas
hc 1-933293-06-3, $30.95, 292p
tpb 1-933293-08-X, $16.95, 292p

Experience Westermead's awakening season by season, the lush heat of summer's passion and the retreat into winter's desolate embrace. Come celebrate and mourn with the people of Westermead as they make their way through a world steeped in beauty and dread.

Fugue XXIX, Forrest Aguirre
hc 1-933293-07-1, $29.95, 220p
pb 1-933293-12-8, $15.95, 220p

These tales come to you from the fringe of speculative literary fiction where innovative minds keep busy dreaming up the future's uncharted territories and mining forgotten treasures of the past. Anything can happen, and does, with regularity.

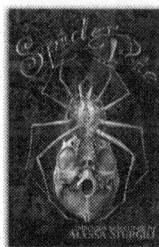

Spider Pie, Alyssa Sturgill
tpb 1-933293-05-5, $10.95, 104p

Sturgill's debut firmly establishes her as the *enfant terrible* of contemporary surrealism. Laden with gothic horror sensibilities, *Spider Pie* is a one-way trip down a rabbit hole inhabited by sexual deviants and friendly monsters, fairytale beginnings and hideous endings.

100 Jolts: Shockingly Short Stories
Michael A. Arnzen
tpb 0-9745031-2-6, $12.95, 156p

This collection features 100 short shots of fiction guaranteed to stun. From his hilarious satire on technical manuals, "Stabbing for Dummies," to his series of "Skull Fragments" vignettes Arnzen proves he has honed his craft to deliver the highest voltage using the fewest words.

www.ingramcontent.com/pod-product-compliance
Lightning Source LLC
Chambersburg PA
CBHW021015180626
46814CB00003B/1296